Forty Beads

The Simple, Sexy Secret for
Transforming Your Marriage

CAROLYN EVANS

D0036335

RUNNING PRESS
PHILADELPHIA · LONDON

Books published by Running Press are available at special discounts for bulk
purchases in the United States by corporations, institutions, and other organizations.
For more information, please contact the Special Markets Department at the Perseus
Books Group, 2300 Chestnut Street, Suite 200, Philadelphia, PA 19103, or call
(800) 810-4145, ext. 5000, or e-mail special.markets@perseusbooks.com.

ISBN 978-0-7624-3928-7
Library of Congress Control Number: 2010049264

E-book ISBN 978-0-7624-4226-3

9   8   7   6   5   4   3   2   1
Digit on the right indicates the number of this printing

Cover photograph by Joshua McDonnell
Design by Joshua McDonnell
Edited by Jennifer Kasius
Typography: Avenir, Bembo, and Helvetica

Running Press Book Publishers
2300 Chestnut Street
Philadelphia, PA 19103-4371

Visit us on the Web!
www.runningpress.com

The opinions and expressions contained in this book are based on the
author's experiences and beliefs and may not work for everyone. The
author and publisher do not guarantee or represent that the method
described herein will benefit everyone and are in no way liable for any use
or misuse of the material.

Love does not consist in gazing at each other,
but in looking together in the same direction.

—ANTOINE DE SAINT-EXUPÉRY

CONTENTS

Introduction

During a bleak mid-January week, with my marriage poised for a downward spiral alongside the economy, I tried to come up with a fantastic 40th birthday present for my husband. Completely by accident, I stumbled across an idea that evolved into something big enough to rock my husband's birthday *and* save my marriage—it's called The Forty Beads Method.

Forty Beads is all about The Forty Beads Method—what it is, why it works, and exactly how to use it to create lasting, positive changes in your relationship. In a nutshell, The Forty Beads Method is a sweet little token system that gets rid of all that nasty negative tension that builds up around sex (specifically, the frequency with which it does or does not occur) and replaces it with the sex life you always thought you should have, which in turn creates the relationship you've always wanted. It works by magically harnessing that easy feeling of connectedness that follows a roll in the hay and *using* that energy to continually benefit your relationship.

Who knew this was possible? Not me. I didn't set out to discover a whole new way of approaching sex in my marriage. The Method evolved as I back-pedaled on my ridiculous offer to give my husband 40 straight days of sex for his 40th birthday. He was concerned about missing days if he pulled a hamstring or something, and I really wasn't sure I had the stamina it would take to go that kind of distance with the deed. So instead of 40 straight days of sex, he got 40 tokens—Beads, actually—each one good for one roll in the hay. That's how it all started, and it's changed our lives—for the better and in a big way. The Beads have even changed how I feel about sex. The Forty Beads Method creates a situation where, for the first time in our marriage, my husband and I are on the same page sexually. Bet you didn't think that was a possibility, did you? Well, it is.

I have a big mouth, and of course I told all my friends about it. Some were immediately intrigued and wanted to get Beading right away. Others were horrified at first but came around to the idea over time after seeing the difference it has made in my marriage. Then I started thinking, why Bead in a vacuum? I already had all these solo Beaders out there checking in with me on a regular basis. Why not get women Beading in groups? It started with a local Bead club in my hometown and has expanded from there. Women getting together, drinking wine, laughing, and supporting each other as they deepen their relationships using The Forty Beads Method.

There are some specific rules of Beading that I call "The Forty Beads Creed" along with some important do's and don'ts, but really, The Forty Beads Method is fun, simple to use, and it produces profound, lasting results. This book offers a new angle on something you already know—that sex is a critical ingredient in the recipe of a successful marriage—and a creative approach for pulling it to the front burner of your marital cooktop. *Forty Beads* does not dispense advice on the actual deed. (Plenty of other books do that.) It's all about getting you to the sheets (not about what you do once you get there) and, in the process, developing the kick-ass marriage you deserve.

Throughout this book I will be referring to heterosexual marriage. This is because the heterosexual marriage is what I know best and absolutely not because I wish to exclude homosexual couples from these pages or The Forty Beads Method. The Method assumes a disparity that often exists between the male and female libidos and offers a way to close that gap. I know that the same disparity can and does exist with some homosexual couples. And although to date, I haven't had a same-sex couple take The Forty Beads Method for a test drive, it is my hope that The Method will offer the same transformational experience for homosexual couples who struggle with conflicting sex drives.

The Forty Beads Method is for you if you love your husband (I'm going to use the word "husband" throughout this book, but feel free to substitute life partner, lover, UPS man—whatever) and want to stay married to him, but you maybe don't like him very much lately or the *like* comes and goes (a lot). The Forty Beads Method is for you if you have this nagging feeling that things could be way better, that your relationship is missing something, and/or you're an *American Idol* junkie who stays up much later than your husband to see which wannabe rocker will flash in the pan next. The Forty Beads Method is definitely for you if your husband walks around with one eyebrow at an angle and forms a full-on "V" when he looks at you, but you can't figure out why he's so pissed since there's really no time for sex—what with doing laundry, taking care of the kids, *and* making dinner. Here's a hint, ladies: The house can be a total wreck and the baby shirtless in a sagging wet diaper, but if he's getting laid regularly, he's cool with it. *All of it.* Because there's one thing that's more important to your husband than everything else combined, multiplied by ten and raised to the fourth power: SEX.

The Forty Beads Method is not for you if you're committed to the status quo and have little or no interest in change. The Forty Beads Method is not for you if your husband is your soul's twin and he *gets you* all the time, without exception, and you never experience any confusion, anger, or guilt associated with sex. By the way, if that's your situation, you two make up part of the .0002% of all relationships. You have uncovered the Holy Grail of couplehood, that which the rest of us dream about and bust our asses trying to achieve. I'd just like to say, from all of us who haven't gotten there yet, "Congratulations. Oh, and we hate you." Finally, The Forty Beads Method is not for you if you're married to a complete asshole or a total douche bag. It happens. Find a different book, and get out as quick as you can.

When you read my story, you'll understand how The Forty Beads Method evolved quite organically. I'm a town crier of sorts and not easily convinced of much, so if I find something that works, whether it's hair gel or yoga pants that suck my butt in and up, I want everybody to know about it. I wrote this book because I just had to tell you. Because I suspect that what works for me, my friends, and my fellow Beaders just might do the trick for you, too.

In Part 1, I'll tell you the story of how I stumbled across 40 Venetian beads that changed my life and my marriage in a big way. The rest of the book will be all about The Forty Beads Method. I'm a fan of books with crystallized nugget chapters, and I want *Forty Beads* to be something you can read a chapter of while waiting in the carpool line and then shove between the seats when the kids get in the car. So, over the course of 40 short chapters, I'll explain all the reasons why The Forty Beads Method works, how it works, and what you can expect if you decide to get the Beads working for you. I'm going to assume that you're a little like me and at first blush will be somewhat freaked out by what these 40 Beads represent. That's okay, but hear me out in Part 2 (Sex: The Deal) on what I believe snags a lot of marriages and why it really is a big deal. I figure you'll probably want some hard facts—maybe even some scientific data—to back up what

I'm putting out there, so Part 3 (Just the Facts, Ma'am) is full of that. In Part 4 (Sex as Commerce), I'll explain how sex in a marriage acts a lot like a commodity and why The Forty Beads Method isn't such a crazy idea. Part 5 (Getting Your Bead On) is the how-to portion of the book—it's all about getting busy with the Beads and the rules of fair play. In Part 6 (The Beadefits), I'll explain why The Forty Beads Method really is worth the trouble and tell you all about the big shift that happens from the moment you put your Beads into action. Because I didn't think you should just take my word for it, throughout the book I've included the experiences of my fellow Beaders—amusing anecdotes, white-knuckle moments, and reasons why they believe in the power of the Bead.

Part 1

A Sexy Little Wives' Tale

I'll just start at the beginning. My husband's birthday was fast approaching. The big 4–0. And even though he wouldn't admit it, I knew Ray had been building this birthday up in his head for at least 20 years. He'd dropped some hints. He mentioned a watch upgrade, showed me a picture of some nerdy-looking telescope he thought he'd like to have for his office even though he'd never shown the slightest bit of interest in stargazing. Nothing seemed to be the right thing, and I just couldn't get behind buying some superfluous item that would be tossed into his toy collection. Particularly during these wobbly economic times, it didn't feel right to throw a big wad of cash at my husband's 40th birthday. That, and the fact that we hadn't really been getting along all that well.

The months leading up to my husband's birthday hadn't been all that great for us. Not awful, but not great. I would say my husband and I had a general lack of interest in each other. Which I figured was fine, given the loads of necessary shit that needed dealing with on any given day. Instead of having a drink together before dinner the way we used to do, I'd be well into my first glass of wine, cooking in the kitchen, when he got home from work. He'd come in, say "Hey," offer a quick smile, and go off to find the kids. We were like two toddlers engaged in parallel play, bobbing along in two separate orbs, doing our own thing. After a family dinner, we'd spin off again, usually to opposite ends of the house.

Or we'd set into fighting. Sometimes knock-down, drag-outs and other times just seething comments followed by periods of silence. We'd go to sleep pissed off, only to wake up and do it all over again the next day. This was how we operated for a while, and I really wasn't all that concerned because I loved my husband, in spite of all the petty bullshit we'd been wading through at that time. I was sure that whatever we were going through would pass and we'd get back on track eventually.

But it turns out he was super-pissed and had been for a while. One afternoon, I was running errands, getting ready for weekend guests (when you live in Charleston, South Carolina, you have a lot of weekend guests) when he called me. We chatted as usual, ticking items off the "you'll do/I'll do" list, and just as I was pulling up to Bed, Bath and Beyond, he laid it on me.

"What are we doing?" he asked.

"I told you. I'm going to Bed, Bath and Beyond, then to the grocery store, then I'm picking up the kids," I said, gathering my stuff to get out of the car.

"No, I mean . . . I can't live like this anymore. I think maybe we should take a break—from each other."

I was immediately defensive and I'm sure I said something like, "What the hell do you mean?" It spiraled down from there on a cold January afternoon in a shopping center parking lot. Turns out, what I called a "temporary bump in the road" was more like a rather large fault line in our marriage. Shit. I tried my best to quell the situation following my knee-jerk defensive attack, but as I cited reasons why I thought we were fine, I realized something had to be done.

During our 13 years of marriage, we had been in this kind of place before. Back when I was performing a lot with my band and keeping crazy-late hours, our marriage slipped beneath the watery surface of an almost loveless state. It was so openly bad that our friends and family braced themselves for the unraveling that so often follows this kind of misery. But eventually, we pushed off the bottom of the pool, thanks to a ton of couples' therapy (spread among at least five highly trained and well-meaning therapists) and a little advice from my sister-in-law.

"Have sex with him every day," she'd said to me late one night when we were up drinking wine.

"What? Are you crazy? No way, man. I'm pretty sure he hates me anyway," I told her.

"Just try it. It worked for us. At least for a while," she'd said.

On the one hand, I was pretty sure I hated him as much as I suspected he hated me. On the other hand, I really wanted to stay married to him, because I knew deep down that he wasn't the asshole he'd pretended to be over the previous year; somewhere in there was that guy I was so obsessed with in my early 20s and left my cushy job in London to be with. Also, there was this precious five-year-old girl involved. In short, I was willing to try *anything*, and having sex with him every day seemed to fall into that category. It worked like a charm. It didn't go on forever (because who has that kind of energy?), but it was like attaching a set of jumper cables to our marriage, and it got us cruising again.

Fast-forward from there to a couple of nights before my husband's big birthday. I knew I was flirting with disaster as the hours lurched dangerously close to the big day and I remained gift-less with no promising prospects. There I stood at the bathroom sink going through my nightly cleansing ritual, when a bit of long-suppressed information emerged: Every year, at least for as long as I've been aware of it, my mom has given my dad an entire month of sex for his birthday. I hadn't really given their *steamy Septembers* much thought until then. Actually, I'd probably put a fair amount of effort into *not* putting my brain around that whole thing, but when I realized I could go from deep in the hole to better than flush in an instant without having to pay for expedited shipping, I decided *what the hell.* What's one month? I was a little drunk (which made my split-second decision almost effortless), and since I was fairly sure my marriage was headed for a nosedive, I marched into the bedroom to make an announcement. Piecing together a few tangled memories and loose assumptions while pulling on my faded cotton pajamas and slathering on hand cream, I heard *It* tumble out of my mouth.

"You're getting 40 straight days of sex for your birthday!"

I probably could've timed the whole thing a little better by making my decree *after* removing the "scary-brown-peel-your-face-off lotion" he and the kids are afraid will eat them alive if they touch. Nonetheless, he responded with appropriate measures of shock, jubilation, and gratitude. Minutes later, though, as he sat back in bed and pondered his good fortune, he started to question just how the whole "every single day for 40 days" thing would work. The look on his face turned from celebration to a mix of trepidation and fear. As I sat next to him reading in bed, he started looking at me like he was staring down the length of a six-foot-long Italian sub sandwich. And he had to eat the *whole thing*.

"So . . . Every. Single. Day. For 40 days. Really?" he asked.

"That's right," I said, flipping through my magazine.

"What if I get sick and miss a day or pull a hamstring or something? What happens then? Do those days just get wasted?" he asked.

"Wasted. Yes. Sorry, that's just my policy. And, look, it's okay if you want to exchange your present for a bunch of personal trainer sessions or something," I told him.

"Oh no! I like my present. I *love* my present. When does it start?" he asked, nervous that his present was about to get yanked and inching over to my side of the bed.

"Uh . . . on your birthday, goodnight!" I said and reached across him to turn out the light.

The next day, I woke to that dreaded feeling I sometimes get the morning after a dinner party where there was lots of good wine and intimate conversation. That nagging feeling I'd said something I shouldn't have, had told too much (one of my worst habits), and would hear it repeated back to me before my coffee. And then I remembered. Forty times. Dammit! In 40 days! That is a lot of sex. I don't care who you are—even if you're part of Hef's harem living at the Playboy Mansion.

As I walked to the bathroom, I reflected on the evening's conversation. I could see why my husband had been taken aback once he felt the weight of this gift I'd laid on him. Forty times in 40 days. In the harsh morning light, I couldn't figure out why I'd come up with such a generous figure, despite the fact he'd been alive that many years. Maybe I shouldn't have counted those years when I didn't even know him yet. I really do have such a big mouth, and once again, it'd worked me into a tight little corner. But seeing as I do have some sense of honor, I do love my man, and I was not about to take back the only gift I had to give, I resolved it was up to me to figure out how to make this thing work.

After getting the kids off to school, I came back to my desk and wracked my brain trying to come up with a way to give the gift some kind of added value, really take it over the top on the big day. I decided to send him on a scavenger hunt on the afternoon of his birthday. Only I'd never done anything like that before, and I didn't want to copy some silly scheme I could find on the Internet. Given that I possess the logistical skills of a slow two-year-old, it took some doing, but I eventually hatched a plan. I would deposit envelopes all over downtown that he would have to retrieve. The envelopes would contain a message, directions on where to go next and a piece of a puzzle. And the puzzle would be a picture of . . . well, me.

I thought about what I should wear in the picture that would become the puzzle. The obvious choice was nothing, but I'm not *that* comfortable with my body since my nipples bear a striking resemblance to number two pencil erasers—on steroids. They're a little gift left over from motherhood and 11 months of nursing the wrong way. I was a punch-drunk, love-struck fool for my baby girl and chose to ignore the sage advice of my mother.

"Hon, you sure you want to let her pull on you like that?" my mom had offered.

"It's okay, Mom. I'm sure they'll go back like they were. I know you don't understand since you never nursed me, but I love everything about being a mother," I'd said. What an idiot.

The full frontal thing was definitely not happening. So I decided I'd have to go to the really fancy lingerie store downtown. They would have just the thing. But first things first. It was the middle of January, and let's just say that bikini line maintenance had not been a top priority for me during those frosty months. I was lucky enough to get an appointment that very morning with Angelica. I liked the sound of her name. It somehow implied less pain for me.

Once at the spa, I thumbed through a couple of old magazines and decided to fix myself some herbal tea that I wouldn't drink. When Angelica came into the relaxation chamber to fetch me, I knew I had the hook-up. Large in size and spirit, everything about her said she was up to the task that lay ahead. She instructed me to strip down and tossed me a washcloth the size of a postage stamp to cover myself with, which I tried—from lots of angles—to do.

Once on the table with Angelica, I started talking. Nonstop. This is what I do during awkward vaginal situations like pap smears and waxings. I told her all about my plans for the scavenger hunt, and she was so inspired, she planned to do the same for her man the following month. I inquired about how business had been lately. Was it likely to pick up with Valentine's Day around the corner? I learned that lots of girls have Angelica fashion designs like hearts and initials special for Valentine's Day. I was impressed but not convinced that a "signature look" was what I needed down there. After the waxing, I surveyed her fine work. She tossed me some "calming cream" and closed the door behind her. I pulled on my jeans (ouch!) and headed for the fancy lingerie shop.

It was really quiet in there and seemingly deserted, so I jangled the bell on the door again to re-announce my arrival. An attractive sales girl looked up from behind the counter. It wasn't that she was unaware of my presence; she just didn't care that I was there. I smiled and fondled some of the silky pieces, winced at the bra prices and was starting to feel like Julia Roberts in *Pretty Woman* when she's getting ignored in that store on Rodeo Drive the day before the spending frenzy.

"Uh, excuse me," I said leaning against the glass counter. "I need an outfit. Well, not just an outfit. I need some kind of 'bad girl been out whoring all night' outfit. It's my husband's 40th and . . . " I said.

And out of nowhere appeared the grande dame of the place, her long hair flowing and stilettos clicking down the marble staircase. She whipped a few strands away from her beautiful face and turned to me.

"Say no more. We'll get you looking like the biggest whore on King Street in no time," she said.

"Oh, thank you!" I said, flitting into a dressing room.

She returned with a sexy little number complete with a garter belt and thigh highs. "Do I have to get some of those fuzzy slippers to wear? I just don't think I'll get much use out of those, you know, later," I explained.

"Oh no. A nice pair of FMP's will do just fine," she said.

"What?" I asked, a little slow on the uptake. "Ohhhh, fuck-me pumps! Got it. Thanks."

I signed the ticket and was on to my next stop—Worthwhile, my favorite boutique in town, my home away from home. And just as I'd hoped, there was my friend Brad behind the counter. He is my beacon of style, my finder of all things cool and the only man in my life who fears no repercussions when he agrees that cigarette pants just aren't a good look for me. A single wag of his extended index finger has the power to free me from the clutches of any unfortunate trend and right my fashion course for long-term wearability.

I slid into the store. "Are you ready for this?" I asked.

Without another word, I pulled out my little sexies one by one and spread them on the counter.

"Oh. Oh. Wow. Wow!!!" he said, bending over and covering his mouth when I got to the garter belt.

I filled him in on the birthday surprise. "I'm gonna need your help," I said.

"Uh, I don't think you're gonna need anybody's help with that outfit, missy," Brad said.

"Well, the thing is . . . I need a picture of me *in* this and I brought my camera and I was thinking maybe . . . " I said looking over toward the dressing rooms.

"What? No way! Girl, you know the lighting sucks in our dressing rooms. You're always complaining about it," he said. He's quick on his feet, but I could see little beads of sweat collecting on his forehead.

"Dammit! You're right. Okay, you're off the hook for that," I agreed. "You know what else I need?" I asked, surveying the giftie items on the shelves. "I need 40 of something. It can be anything."

"What?" he said, looking confused.

"Okay, I gave Ray 40 straight days of sex for his birthday," I confessed.

"What? Oh my God! You vixen!" Brad howled.

"I know! It's crazy, right? And I don't want to end up in the hospital or something so then I thought it'd be better if we worked some kind of token system. I mean, every single day for 40 days is just too much, right? I don't know what I was thinking," I said.

"Okay, you are *killing me*, but you know I'll do anything to help a guy get laid!" He fished around in the underneath cabinets and pulled out a dusty Mason jar full of beads. "Here. Take these

Venetian beads—we got them on a buying trip in Italy a long time ago. They've been hanging around forever," Brad explained handing over The Beads.

"Sweet! You're the best!" I said, hugging the Beads. We air-kissed, and I headed home.

On the way there, I tried to think of which friend I would torture with the task of taking my semi-nude shots. The problem was that I needed it done, like, that minute. As I pulled into my driveway, I noticed that Ludmilla, my occasional housekeeper, was still there, probably waiting on the towels to dry so she could fold them and leave. I couldn't ask her to do it. Could I?

"Ludmilla!" I called coming in the door. "You busy?"

The "shoot" went pretty well, except that Ludmilla kept encouraging me to smile and well, I wanted to look a little more Victoria's Secret than that. We finally got a marginally okay picture and I scampered back upstairs cradling my camera.

I thanked Ludmilla profusely, sweetened her check, and went to print up my picture, grateful that my mom had given my daughter a handy photo printer for her birthday. As the printer spat me out legs first, I was pleased to see that the flash had taken care of my blotchy red bikini line but then horrified when the whole photo plopped into the tray. My eyes were solid red. Like a devil. All I needed was a pair of horns and a tail.

As much as I hated to do it, I had to go to the photo shop. Lucky for me, I was pretty adept at the self-service kiosk, so I got there and went straight to work. Only there was this pesky college student/photo lab assistant who kept hovering and asking if I needed any help.

"Nope. I got it, thanks," I said with one arm cradling the big machine.

Next, I flew back home to create the *me puzzle* and assemble the envelopes. Have you ever taken a pair of scissors and sliced up an image of your scantily clad self? Well, it's just not a natural thing to do, and it creeped me out, since it seems like something a serial killer would get a thrill out of doing. I stuffed each envelope with a little piece of me and a scavenger hunt clue. Well, they weren't really clues, more like directives on where to go next and what to do there. I didn't have time for rhyming riddles or dirty limericks. Late on the afternoon before Ray's birthday, I ran all over the city depositing sealed envelopes and enlisting the help of barkeeps and sales assistants—mostly complete strangers—to create a scavenger hunt that I hoped would rock my husband to his very core.

Over and over, I went through my whole song and dance about the big birthday, the scavenger hunt and how great it would be, if they didn't mind too much—blah blah blah— tucking this envelope behind the register for my man. Some folks were totally inspired by my creative idea; others, not so much. Lucky for me, people thinking I'm a complete idiot doesn't upset me. It usually just spurs me on because I know if I'm fired up *enough* about something and perform the tricked-out, extended version of my old soft-shoe routine, I can eventually pull even the most annoyed listener over to my cause. Exhausting? Yes. But oddly satisfying.

First, there were the guys behind the bar at our favorite French brasserie, complete with a tiny tiled floor, cozy wood-walled banquettes, and antiqued mirrors announcing the menu. Unfortunately for me, my favorite bartender, Smoak, who always presents me with my special jumbo glass of Chardonnay as I approach the bar, wasn't there. That would have been too easy—he really likes Ray and would've been all too happy to set things up. Instead, I got the really bored afternoon shift who, despite my best efforts, were only marginally sure that they could pass the envelope to my man along with the shots I bought when he showed up the next day.

Next, I went to the wine shop, where the Irish manager, looking like he'd just come off the football field in his knee socks and cleats, was easy to convince. I learned from my previous stop that it is way better to go the purchase-before-request route, so I bought a top-shelf selection for him to present to Ray and *then* began my explanation and request. He was happy to oblige and poured me a couple fingers of red wine, which I gratefully knocked back before pressing on. Next, I dropped an envelope with the ladies at the lingerie shop.

After that, I ran back to Worthwhile because I decided it would be kind of hilarious if Brad handed the Beads over to Ray—you know, add another element of intrigue. I put them inside an envelope that looked just like the others and sealed it up tight. Of course, Brad was cracking up as he tucked the beads under the register and promised to keep an eye out for handsome Ray the next day. The envelope with the Beads also gave the last directive, which was to proceed to this sweet hotel about 30 minutes outside of town, where I would be waiting.

The afternoon of his birthday, I didn't take his calls. He didn't need to talk to me. I had busted my ass the day before making sure of that. And when I was sure that the scavenger hunt was under way, I headed out to the hotel. I dropped the final envelope at the front desk, which held the last and sexiest piece of the *me puzzle* and a room key. I got settled in the room, put some fine champagne on ice, and was feeling pretty pleased with myself until I realized I had forgotten the stinking fuck-me pumps. I felt a little less sexy and a lot less statuesque (actually, statuesque is a stretch for me even in towering stilletos) walking around the hotel room in my stocking feet, but short of talking the concierge out of her sensible navy heels, I was out of luck and decided that would have to be okay.

I got all strapped in and up, and just so you know, garter belts are a pain in the ass. They go *under* your thong. Who knew? The ladies at the lingerie shop knew and set me straight in short order. I felt like a high-priced whore waiting around for a client. Robe on. Robe off. TV on. TV off. I was bored, so of course, I started drinking. Finally, there was a knock at the door. It was my half-drunk, *very* excited husband with a handful of envelopes, and a really big grin on his face. The evening progressed just like evenings of that type should. The scavenger hunt did, in fact, rock my husband to his very core and even threw off his sense of balance for a few days. The next morning, drinking coffee in our plush bathrobes, Ray was scrambling the *me puzzle* and putting it back together again when he came across the Beads.

"So, wait a minute. What the hell are these for?" he asked. "Brad wouldn't tell me when he gave them to me, but he said he thought I'd like them."

"Oh! Yeah. Remember how I said I was giving you 40 straight days of sex for your birthday? Well, I thought a token system might work better—that's what the Beads are for," I explained. "I'm gonna put a bowl by my bed and every time you want to have sex, you just drop a Bead in my bowl and that's how I'll know you're ready."

"So, when I want to *do it*, I just give you a Bead. Really?" he seemed skeptical.

"Yeah. That works, right? We'll figure out all the details along the way," I said.

"Really," he said pondering the thought and then glazing over with delight. "Well, all right!"

And so it has gone on from there and has changed everything about our life together in a pretty profound way. What started out as a half-baked, over-zealous idea had morphed into a token system, which evolved into the full-blown Forty Beads Method, and is steadily making married life better for couples who try it. Life is just easier and a whole lot more fun with The Forty Beads

Method. Even when the hard stuff pops up (because it inevitably does), we're ready for it and deal with it better as a couple, because the Beads keep us connected to each other. That may sound all saccharine-sweet, but it's just practical. I'm not a sentimental gal, I'm just after what works—for me and for my fellow Beaders—and The Forty Beads Method is just that.

Part 2

Sex: The Deal

1
......
Men Love Sex

Let's get something straight from the start: Men love sex. More than anything. They have to have it and if they're not getting it, they think they're dying. That's just how it is. You can gnash your teeth about it all you want (we all have) but that won't change a thing. It's been that way, like, forever, which is probably why Eve tried to cover herself with fig leaves—so Adam would just lay off.

And they think about it all the time. *All* of the time. Except when they're sneezing. I know you've heard the ridiculous numbers about how often a man thinks about sex. Something like 960 times a day, but I've also heard it said that they only think about it once—for 24 hours. Or all day, and then they dream about it all night. And we have to assume sex is what gets them out of bed in the morning. I mean, who hasn't lazily rolled over and been inadvertently stabbed by the blue steel? It's a little startling, to say the least. And there's little doubt that sex is how he prefers to end his day. (Ever get the tap, tap, tap—just at that delicious, most beautiful moment when you're falling asleep?) The evidence is overwhelming: Men love sex and for most of them, it's their favorite thing in the whole wide world.

2

· · · · · ·

Men and Sex and Trouble

We all know that sex can get a man into a heap o' trouble. I could cite examples of bad choices that men I know have made, but that wouldn't be a smart thing for me to do. Besides, you don't have to look farther than your television to see great examples of politicians, professional athletes, and other celebrity types valiantly impaling themselves on the sex sword. Sex or the possibility of sex will take a man down faster than anything else in this world. Greed can wreck a guy's life pretty good too, but illicit sexual activity can torch his world in the time it takes to strike the match.

And this is nothing new. Think of Odysseus and those sexy Sirens. He'd heard about the sailors who'd lost their shit and crashed their ships on the rocks just trying to get a glimpse of those sneaky little vamps. And I really don't think those sailors were wanting to grab a cup of coffee and discuss the latest trends in Greek architecture. No, they were all, "Man, they sound good. I bet they look good too. We got to get us some of that." And just like that, they'd tossed over their dreams of riches or victory of whatever they were sailing for, in favor of the possibility of some nookie. But not Odysseus. He was too smart for that. He was quite aware of the mighty pull that sex has on a man and the deadly trouble it can cause, so he stuffed his crew's ears full of wax and ordered them to strap his ass to the ship's mast so they stood a fair chance of making safe passage past the Sirens' calls.

Men love sex and will do whatever they need to do to get some. It's like a gravitational pull toward what they want, and sometimes there's nothing in this world big enough to stand in a man's way—not the possibility or even the certainty of gutting his own life. I'm not looking to trash the opposite sex here, but how many powerful women can you name who've tossed away their position in their family and the world over some torrid affair? Take your time compiling your list—I'll wait. Yeah, I couldn't think of any either. Interesting, don't you think?

3

......

Sex: His Magic Elixir of Life

Men. God bless 'em and I love 'em because they're just not that complicated. My psychologist friend, Bill Moon, has been working with couples for more than 40 years, and he says that men have only three states of being: *okay*, *not okay*, and *pissed*. Bill says that when a man's *not okay*, all he wants to do is get back to *okay*. Not having sex with your husband? That puts him into the *not okay* category. And he won't spend a lot of time in that *not okay* place before he moves right on over to *pissed*. While there are lots of events and situations that can hurl a man headlong into the *not okay* state, there is one thing that offers your man the quickest, most direct route back to Okaysville. That's right. Sex. For lots of reasons (we'll get into exactly what some of them are later) sex seems to pull a man back to his center, that *okay* place we all prefer to be.

One thing we women know, but don't really like to examine, is the fact that sex makes men *feel* better. They tell us all the time how important sex is to them, but we're not likely to listen since the message is usually tangled up with the additional complaint that they're just not getting enough of it. I don't know about you, but any information that is conveyed to me in a hostile or whiny fashion gets dismissed immediately. So maybe we don't like hearing it directly from our men, but it is nonetheless true that if they are ailing in any way, most men are pretty sure that sex will heal them. And this isn't a message that's been shrouded in mystery over the ages—it's been out there forever. Just think of the song "Sexual Healing" by the late, oh-so-great Marvin Gaye. I can't print the lyrics here, but the name says it all. Have you ever really listened to the words? He's got to, got to have it because it just makes him *feel* better—if not spectacular. And better is . . . well, it's better, right? And not just for him—for everybody else hanging around him. Men get ornery when they don't have sex. I bet there's some kind of dry spell/meanness ratio that some brilliant female mathematician somewhere has worked out. A man's irritability rises steadily, if not exponentially, as time passes without sex or the real possibility of sex in the very near future.

A question. Is there anything that raises your level of satisfaction with your relationship more than an hour-long therapy session where your husband totally understands you and celebrates *all* that you are? Maybe I'm assuming that everyone has spent as much time working on their relationship as my husband and I have, but who doesn't know that exhilarating feeling of walking out of your therapist's office hand in hand on a beautiful sunshiny day and feeling that all is right with your marriage and your world? Well, that's how your husband feels right after having sex. It. Completes. Him. Not only do men *want* sex, they truly believe that they *need* sex. To survive. They think of it as the answer, the cure, the magic elixir of life. And just because sex may not be what *we* need to fill us up or make us whole, doesn't make it any less true for them. We don't have to understand it or agree with it, but if we choose to live with a man in a romantic way, we sure do have to deal with it—one way or another.

4

······

Why Holding Out Doesn't Work

As I've said, for a guy, sex is number one, the whole enchilada and then some. And ladies, let me tell you, your husband wants to have sex with you. Even if you've gotten slack with your bikini line maintenance. Even if you haven't shucked that baby weight. Sex is what he loves better than anything. Better than football and better than drinking with the guys. Here's the thing: If you're withholding that one thing he values most in this world, and I say this with a lot of love, he hates you. He might not come out and say it, and he probably feels real bad about it, but he hates you.

Now, I'm sure there are things that he loves about you. Maybe you're a gourmet cook, maybe you make him laugh, and maybe you two are raising some wonderful kids together. Those things are great and can keep a marriage going—for a while. I know this may sound sexist and maybe even too simple an argument to put out there, since relationships are so complicated, but the bottom line is, if you're holding out in the sex department, your marriage is headed for the crapper. I know. I've held out and watched mine circle the bowl a few times.

So why do we hold out? Lots of reasons. We hold out because there's something we want that we're not getting (like good husband behavior), and we hold out because we're getting too much of something we don't want (like bad husband behavior). And while we're holding out, we turn a blind eye to the fact that what we're doing isn't getting us any closer to what we want—it's actually just widening the gap between what we have and what we want—assuming that a healthy, happy relationship is what we're after. Don't you know couples where the wife continuously berates and criticizes her husband's behavior? Despite her accomplished (albeit bitchy) efforts, he never changes his behavior, does he? That's because you can't browbeat good behavior into a person. And by the same token, you can't withhold sex from your husband and realistically expect his behavior to change in a positive way. I know, we think that at some point, he'll wake up, *get it* that we're holding out because we're pissed and then decide to straighten up and fly right. It just never works out that way, though, does it? In fact, just the opposite happens—they start misbehaving even more—just to spite the bitch who's holding out on them.

Holding out is a flawed and convoluted method that, for all the effort expended, will never deliver the results you want. Who's interested in spinning their wheels for nothing? The Forty Beads Method is about giving you a direct, more efficient route to getting what you want, and unlike holding out, it doesn't involve you tightening up, but instead it involves letting go. And by the way, this tightening up? Not good for you. We'll talk more later about how withholding creates a sense of lack and what that does for him, but your cinching up also creates a sense of depletion in you. Who wants that? I mean, aren't we all seeking a sense of abundance in our lives? It's exhausting wearing that iron-clad chastity belt. *I know*. It uses up a lot of energy that could be pointed in other, more positive, directions.

I was having dinner with my husband one night after we were well into our Beading practice, and what do you know? The subject of sex came up.

I asked, "Was I really that bad about the whole withholding thing? I mean, really *that bad*?"

He said, "We're having such a nice time, let's not talk about that right now."

Well, of course, I couldn't leave it at that. "Tell me," I said. "I want to know."

With both of his hands flat on the crisp white tablecloth, in a low, whispered tone he came out with it: "You were the worst."

Point taken. Hell, I didn't think I was *that* bad, but whatever. I'll own it. "Hello, my name is Carolyn Evans and I'm a recovering withholder." Honestly, it has only been *since* I've experienced the incredible difference that The Forty Beads Method has made in my relationship that I've been able to clearly see, *without a doubt*, how important sex is to a marriage and how destructive withholding it can be. The thought kept dropping into my mind: *Before the Beads, shitty marriage. After the Beads, great marriage.* Huh. That's when it hit me: Sex really *is* the big deal everybody makes it out to be—for better or for worse. Seeing myself as a withholder was sort of a rearview-mirror realization, and by the time my faulty ways came into sharp focus, I was already Beading a path to my best marriage ever.

5

······

Dodging and Weaving

We've all done it. And if I hadn't discovered The Forty Beads Method, I'm sure I'd still be weaving little webs of confusion and distraction to get out of having sex when I don't feel like it. Why do we attempt to elude the sexual advances of our men? I can think of many reasons. Sometimes we avoid sex with them because they've pissed us off, but often it's just because there's something else we'd rather be doing, like sleeping or flossing. But we all know it's inevitable that at some point, even if we don't feel like it, we're going to have to surrender the booty.

One of my best friends says that every so often, her man gets this look in his eye—you know, that crazy grin with one eyebrow half cocked—and when he does, she may as well just go ahead and drop to the kitchen floor. We dodge and weave, and then we give it up. And in the middle of all that pushing and pulling are the games we play—which I think can be funny as shit. You know, those creative yet totally lame excuses we come up with to stave off his sexual advances when we're just not feeling it? What follows are a few really good ones some of my fellow Beaders confessed and reasons why they're so not worth the effort.

❂ THROWING UP A SMOKESCREEN

"I don't want to just do it. Let's wait until we have some time to really make love."

He's so not buying this one. (And by the way, I *hate* the term "making love." It makes me want to hurl.) When you say you want to wait until there's ample time for lovemaking, you're implying that having sex with him is *so* important and meaningful to you. So important and meaningful that you want to put it off? There are a couple of reasons why this excuse will piss him off: (a) because it's crap and he knows it, and (b) because he *does* just want to *do it* and he doesn't give a shit about the whole "making love" thing any more than you do. Sometimes, yes, both parties delight in an extended roll in the hay covering all the bases and tossing in a few extra innings for added pleasure, but generally speaking, sex doesn't have to be this long, drawn-out affair. So postponing sex now in favor of a lengthy sexual encounter on a yet-to-be-determined date? They hate that. Better to just skip the whole not-so-compelling romantic routine and just hop in the sack.

❂ FAKING A YEAST INFECTION

This one's pretty clever and quite effective, when used sparingly. After all, it's not like he's going to want to check things out for himself. Three little words that will send a man packing and on high alert until further notice: *itchy down there.* Which cracks me up, because while they say that it is *technically possible* for a man to contract a yeast infection from a woman who has one, I can't imagine the thing thriving on the tip of a penis like it did in the warm, dark cave where it sprang to life. Conjecture aside, this excuse typically works well because most men wouldn't think of risking it. But there's a downside. You may have to produce a clean Pap report before he'll be ready to go there again. That's a lot of trouble and could even produce some bad karma. Bad karma combined with the stress of keeping up the whole itchy-scratchy charade might be enough to actually bring on that angry beast. Yikes. Totally not worth it.

⊛ PLAYING POSSUM

Being truly (albeit conveniently) asleep when he comes to bed is understandable. It's crazy the kind of ground we cover in a day, and uh, yeah—we get tired. Faking sleep is a different deal, and you're probably not as good at it as you think you are. I've made the mistake of lying listless, but with my mouth tightly closed. That's not realistic. If you're going to play possum, you've got to commit to the role, let your chin drop and your mouth gape open. Not very attractive, but way more believable and yet still unlikely that he'll buy it. Here's why: Playing possum is usually preceded by an allusion to his desire for sex in the near future. I'm sure Meryl Streep could pull off a good possum—it probably has something to do with a slowed breathing pattern and maybe even some drooling—but if you haven't attended the Actor's Studio, I wouldn't be so convinced that your possum is so convincing. And is it really worth the risk of getting caught? I can say from experience that no, no it's not. It's mortifying for everyone involved. He feels like a piece of shit that you'd go to such lengths to avoid having sex with him, and you feel like an asshole for going to such lengths to avoid having sex with him. I'm feeling sheepish just thinking about it.

While some of these techniques are more effective than others, we all know that in the end, there's nothing embarrassing enough or scary enough to pull a man's attention away from the nookie for any significant period of time. So here's something to ponder: What if there wasn't this whole push-and-pull thing going on in your marriage? What if there was a way for everybody to get on the same page and fall into that fun, easy flow—both in and out of the bedroom. There is a way—it's called The Forty Beads Method.

6

•••••

The Rare Husband Theory

It's hard for some of us to absorb this truth about guys and sex. Maybe you don't want to think that your guy is so singularly focused. Sorry! And I know that as women living it up in the 21st century, it's not our primary concern in life to be somebody's sex object. Again, sorry! That's not *all* you are to him, but it just happens to be a rather important piece of what you are to him. Maybe you really don't want this to be true, and you're tempted to say that your husband is different from most guys when it comes to sex. You might even believe that he doesn't really like sex all that much, since you two don't get it on all that often. Have you asked him? I didn't think so. I'm sure there is that very occasional husband out there who doesn't really dig sex. The exception proves the rule. But the chance that you have one of those very rare husbands? Not very likely.

If your man maintains a high level of irritability *and* you've always thought he just didn't like sex, I'm afraid you might not have a rare breed on your hands, but instead just your typical, run-of-the-mill, sex-starved husband. Chances are, the fact that he's not getting any has everything to do with his general pissed-off mood. I know. Not what you wanted to hear, but better you hear it from me in this book instead of across a mahogany conference table in an attorney's office, right? It's just one of those things that on some level we know to be true but try to push out beyond our peripheral vision in hopes that it will somehow dissolve. It won't.

7

Sex or a Dark Chocolate Dove Bar?

Some women love sex—they say they can't get enough of it. Good for them. A portion of these women are also claiming an overactive sex drive to boost their allure at a dinner party or for the cheap thrill of shocking the uptights. I can respect the desire to shake things up (it's one of my favorite pastimes) but I also find these self-professed nymphos a bit irritating, since the rest of us can sometimes feel penned into a defensive little corner when we're not willing to drone on about how much we love, love, love sex. At the other end of the spectrum, you've got a totally different group of women who complain (a lot) about having to have sex with their husbands and how much they hate, hate, hate it. Incidentally, this is a way that a lot of women bond—by bitching about their husbands' overactive libidos—but really, all they're doing (I used to do it, too) is supporting each other in staying at odds with their husbands. Is that helpful? Not really.

You've got your two extremes, but I think most of us fall somewhere in between. We like sex, but we probably crave a lot of other things a lot more. And while we definitely can appreciate all the benefits that the toe-curling, mind-blowing orgasm delivers, we're also okay with a good book, a warm blanket, and a dark chocolate Dove Bar. Does this make us cold bitches? I don't think so. The thing is, for us women, sometimes sex is all starbursts and fireworks, and other times it's just okay. And while we might be unclear on what our outcome will be, there's one thing we know for sure: There's going to be some clean-up involved. Practically speaking, sex can be a pain in the ass. So often we're a little iffy on going through with the deed. Throw in all the other demands placed on our time in any given 24-hour period, and sex easily gets pushed to the tail end of our to-do list or shoved off the list entirely. Often it's nothing personal against our dudes—it's just how things shake out a fair amount of the time.

8

......

Some Kind of Crazy Glue

People say kids are the glue in a marriage. If that's the case, then how come there are so many kids out there with divorced parents? Kids aren't the glue. Raising a family is a blast, and it's also hard as hell. Kids eat up a lot of time and focus—even for the most lackadaisical of parents, much less the obsessed ones. (Don't get me started.) More often than not, our children take our attention *away* from the most important relationship in the family: the married couple, the peeps who got the party started in the first place.

And it's these precious children that often provide the most convenient excuses for why couples don't get it on like they should. Shhh! We don't want to wake the baby! Or later, the 12-year-old across the hall, or even later, the college-age kid home for Christmas break! I am absolutely crazy about both of my children, but it's also true that at times they have sucked the very life out of me. That was literally the case when my daughter was a baby, since I nursed her *way* longer than I should have (thanks again, La Leche League!), became anemic, and looked like a stick figure walking around with this apple-cheeked cherub on my hip.

Like a lot of moms with little kids, sex with my husband was definitely not a priority for me. It's hard to want to have sex when you're getting pawed by a toddler all day and the only alone time you can secure is in the shower. If I remember correctly, I think I probably put out just enough to keep things civil between my husband and me for only a small portion of the time. Coincidentally, I also remember having huge screaming matches with him in our tiny kitchen on Hurst Drive over the most ridiculous stuff, while our baby girl screamed even louder in the background. It was not the most savory time in our marriage, and now I know why. I was so focused on my baby and trying to be the most kick-ass mom ever (I even made my own baby food, which at that time was a pretty weird thing to do) that I forgot to pay attention to what's important in keeping a marriage good. It took a few years of neglect to finally *cut off* the love supply to the relationship, but as I mentioned earlier in my Sexy Little Wives' Tale, our marriage eventually tanked and it took a lot of doing to get it livable again. Kids aren't the glue. It's way more common that those little buggers are what lead us to forget about the glue. I'm not saying sex is the *only* adhesive that's important in keeping a marriage together in a happy way, but it is some kind of super-necessary crazy glue.

9

......

Why Can't We All Just Get Along?

If you think God doesn't have a sense of humor, ponder this for
a moment: A woman has to feel close to her husband in order to
want to have sex with him. Conversely, a man has to have sex
with his wife in order to feel close to her. Quite the conundrum,
right? It sort of feels like a setup, doesn't it? And as a rule, if our
husbands aren't being nice, then we're not going to have sex with
them. We're just not *into* having sex with assholes. And here's
the rub: The more you give him the cold shoulder, the bigger
prick he becomes, creating this vicious negative cycle that self-
perpetuates until you can't even stand the way he breathes. Do I
sound like I know what I'm talking about? I've had some experience with this, and chances are, you have, too.

Marriage can easily turn into a war of the wills, and this has a
lot to do with the fact that men and women come at this *love thing*
from really different places. There are some scientific reasons for
this that we'll explore in Part 3, but when you think about it, it is
pretty crazy that we're expected to partner up and mate for life.
This shit is hard. I bet God stays pretty entertained watching us
down here trying to piece it all together and make it work.

We approach this love thing from really different places, but
in the end, our common goal (whether we realize it or not) is to

enjoy a feeling of connectedness with our partner. As men and women, there are different things that get us there. For us women, there are lots of situations and events that promote a feeling of connectedness and closeness with our husbands, but often, it's the little things that get us—a conversation where *you* talk and *he* hears everything you say, a tender moment observed between him and the kids, or even your husband filling your car up with gas. It's the closeness these types of events create for us that reminds us ladies that things are good, we're being treated right by our husbands, and he's our partner on the same team. If we're feeling this connectedness and having our needs met, we're happy. But if we spend an extended period of time *not* getting our needs met—like say, he *never* pitches in around the house or he's *always* plugged into the TV—that pisses us off. We'll eventually question why we're married to some dude who's not even on the same team. How long it takes us to get seriously irritated depends on the woman; it could take weeks or years, but at some point we'll get our fill of not getting what we need.

Something similar happens for guys when they're not getting their needs met. I think we all know what rests firmly at the top of most every guy's need list. That's right. Sex. For a guy, getting sex on a regular basis translates into "I am loved," which produces the next thought, "I am *exactly* where I need to be," which progresses to "I freaking love my wife." Having sex on a regular basis makes a man feel totally taken care of by his wife and like they're partners on the same team. I suspect that inside the male mind, it's as simple a case as you're either *with him* or you're *against him* when it comes to the sex thing.

Having sex often = you're with him on the same team.

Withholding sex = you're against him and *definitely not* on the same team.

So a guy who's suffering a major sexual dry spell is most likely (even unconsciously) thinking, "I am not getting what I need. I am not loved. This feels bad." This feeling permeates his being in a really negative way and will eventually lead him to the thought, "I am *not* where I need to be." And just like us ladies, it could take months or years, but not getting his needs met will at some point lead him to question his marriage. And what do most guys do when they start to question their marriage? (Don't hate me for pointing out the big smelly elephant that's nosed its way into this discussion.) They (sometimes) start looking around. I know. *Really* not what you wanted to hear, and it would sound so sexist if it weren't coming from me, right? But the truth is that being sexually discontent makes a man vulnerable to an affair or at least some flirty workplace/social situation you wouldn't be thrilled about. That's just how it is. I could apologize for it, but it's not my fault. I have to point it out, because infidelity exists as a real possibility in a sexless marriage—everybody knows that— and failing to acknowledge this fact won't make it go away.

10

......

It's Your Treasure

It's your treasure box. (I know. I couldn't resist the pun.) Everybody knows that. And ladies, we're not living in the Stone Age where the dude would drag his woman back to the cave by her hair whenever he felt a twitch under his loincloth. Actually, they probably didn't make it back to the cave, did they? And we're way past the whole "It's a woman's duty to take care of her husband." The Forty Beads Method is about a choice, *not* a duty (more on that later), and as women living in the free world during the 21st century, we are enjoying the perks that some badass women slugged it out to provide for us. We get to choose *what* we want to do in this world, *who* we want to love, *if* we want to get married, and if so, *when*. Our world is full of choices, so if you have chosen to get married, why not go ahead and *choose* to make your marriage a place where spontaneous wildflowers spring forth instead of a toxic waste dump where negativity breeds contempt? Okay, maybe a little overstated, but you catch my drift. You *do* want to be happy, right? Well, if you're married or in a committed relationship and it sucks, so does your life.

As I said in the introduction of this book, if you messed up and married a total douche, figure out a successful exit strategy and move on. But if you do love your husband and have no plans for leaving the marriage, why not do what you can to make your marriage the best it can be? After all, if your marriage sucks, who's the one suffering? Uh, that would be you (oh yeah, and him and probably the kids, too, if you have them). You're the one who's got to bump up against your own marriage every single day and go to bed with it every single night. Letting your relationship just limp along and barely get by isn't a really fun way to live a life. And did you hear? We're only getting this one life—that's not very many.

So what if I told you that, right now, you are sitting on some really valuable treasure. That's right, you're sitting on it. I apologize for swerving into the raunchy lane, but we all know it's your treasure that he loves more than anything, so why not go ahead and spread the wealth and enjoy all benefits your act of generosity has to offer. In her really insightful book *For Better: The Science of a Good Marriage*, Tara Parker-Pope, author of the *New York Times* "Well" blog, explains that "over time, regular sex can improve your mood, make you more patient, damp down anger and lead to a better, more contented relationship." Who's not interested in those types of upgrades?

The thing is, a marriage is always in motion. We're all the time falling apart and coming back together—that's why they threw in the bit about "for better or for worse" at the ceremony. I know. I totally spaced on that part when I agreed to it, too—I was more concerned with the placement of oceana roses at the reception and my perfectly coiffed up-do. When you get right down to it, every basically sound relationship between two reasonable people has the potential to trace the lines of a never-ending upward helix that keeps getting better and better (with some intermittent dips and plateaus), or to be pulled down into a negative spiral that ends in divorce or at least produces two miserable people. And while there certainly are other factors that can tip the scales in making a marriage better or worse, sex is a really big one. Which brings us back to our multitude of choices. You can choose to make sex something that is freely given or you can snap your legs shut. (Let me know how that works out for you.) The thing is, *who* are you saving it for? Ladies, it's time to love the one you're with—and you can start by surrendering the booty. Or not. It's your choice. And whether we realize it or not, we make these choices every single day. We choose love and rise above what threatens to pull us apart, or we choose to be lazy about it and get passively sucked down into the muck and mire of common, everyday bullshit. The Forty Beads Method helps you make the right choices, and the rest just takes care of itself.

11
......
The Sure Thing

The Forty Beads Method is about you giving your man the key to your treasure box, and let me tell you, from the moment you hand him those Beads, everything changes in a really significant way. When I explained to my husband what the Beads were for, he looked at me as if I were Venus, the Goddess of Love, sailing into the hotel room on a clamshell. Maybe the most astonishing element to emerge from using The Forty Beads Method for me and for tons of other Beaders is that the powerful effect it has on a relationship doesn't wear off—it actually deepens and gets even better, because there are two really happy people hanging out in your marriage.

An important piece of The Forty Beads Method for a guy is that he doesn't have to wonder if he's going to get the Heisman. For those of you who don't have a football-obsessed man, maybe I should clarify what I mean by that term. The Heisman is this big-deal award given to one college football player every year—the one who kicked the most ass on the football field. The actual trophy that the player receives is a cast bronze football player with a ball tucked under one arm and the other arm straight out and open-palmed as if to say, "Back off, you bastards!" The dude on the trophy is defending his post and holding his ground, kind of like how we fend off our husbands when we're not in the mood.

Well, here's the thing. When he starts caterpillaring over to your side of the bed and you say, "Nah, I don't really feel like it tonight," you think, "No big deal, I was just being honest," right? Well, right and wrong. You see, it's all about perspective. While "no big deal" accurately describes the situation from your point of view, his take on it is probably quite different. Getting the Heisman can, and usually does, deliver a crushing blow to your man. And while it may not feel fair or make sense to us, it is nonetheless true that a guy will carry that shove-off around with him for days or until the situation is corrected by a successful sexual encounter. And by the way, getting the Heisman will constellate slightly different feelings in different men, but generally, without many exceptions, it just makes them feel like shit. Sometimes we might have some interest or compassion for the blow our Heisman maneuver delivers our men, and other times, not so much. Interested or not, we still have to deal with this dude sulking around the house dragging a big stinky ball of angst. Is that somebody you're going to want to hang out with? I don't think so.

Since I became a sure thing, my husband doesn't often forget that I rock his world, and for that, he consistently gives me the best version of himself. I love that. I don't know about you, but I can thrive on a steady diet of "best foot forward" husband behavior. And here's the thing, you're getting his best version of himself at home and he's also taking that personal best out into the world. That's always a good thing. We want the men we love to be as successful as they can be, right? One faithful Beader drew some interesting correlations between Beading and her husband's success as a trader in the New York Stock Exchange. She said that they've both noticed that he makes some curiously profitable trades right after they've redeemed a Bead. I love that.

12

······

What Would Gloria Say?

I think maybe I know what you're thinking by now. And yes, it is *your* body and yes, you have the right to do with it what you please. Nobody wants to give away their control or become somebody's sex slave. I agree. And what would Gloria Steinem say about all this? Well, I haven't asked her, but I think she might be cool with it. You see, as women living in the 21st century, we know we hold the key to our own sexual destiny. (She's one of the women we can thank for that.) It's not even something we consciously consider anymore—we've internalized this truth about ourselves. Most of us have moved on past the whole "I am woman, hear me roar" thing. It was a useful mantra and worked well—when we needed it. The sexual revolution was a time for women to separate from the men and put themselves out in front—it was "me" time and it was necessary in order to reach certain goals. What I'm suggesting by way of The Forty Beads Method is that as women, maybe we're ready to move past the "me" and are now just as interested in creating a happy "we"—as in, a thriving partnership with a man. A rejoining that's possible now that there's more equal footing (as far as sex is concerned inside a marriage).

What my fellow Beaders and I have realized is that we're willing to *share* the sexual power, because having a great relationship is way more fun than being the iron-fisted gatekeeper of sex in the marriage. The Forty Beads Method creates a situation where the *relationship* holds the power—not the man or the woman alone. And the relationship gains strength and depth from that power— much more valuable and beneficial strength than either partner could receive from holding the sexual power on their own. So it's not about losing your power, but more about loosening your grip on it and closing in on what you really want. Gloria Steinem is all about empowering women to lead authentic and meaningful lives. Well, having a successful marriage, for the women who choose to pair up with a man, is definitely a major piece of the brain-teasing puzzle of life. So yes, I think Gloria would dig The Forty Beads Method. But just in case she hates it, I don't think I'll ask her.

13

••••••

One Big Love Triangle

The Forty Beads Method is *not* about either you *or* your husband
holding the sexual power. Instead, it's about giving that power to
the relationship and watching the relationship gain strength and
thrive from that power—which in turn delivers lots of good
things back to you and your husband. The Method is all about
feeding the relationship, and when that happens, everybody gets
what they want. You become one big joyful trinity—you, your
husband, and your relationship. You are both part of your relationship, but separate from it also, and when you view it this way,
it makes sense why it's important to feed the relationship and
keep it healthy, right? The Forty Beads Method creates this big
love triangle between you, your husband, and your relationship,
with the relationship hanging out at the top of the triangle. You
see, the relationship has to be at the top—as the priority—
because it's the container that holds you two together.

The Forty Beads Method helps you create your own little
mutually beneficial love triangle where you and your husband
continuously feed your relationship and your relationship, in turn,
feeds the two of you. I don't really learn very well from charts or
graphs, but in this case, I thought a visual aid might make sense.
See the next page. Cool, right?

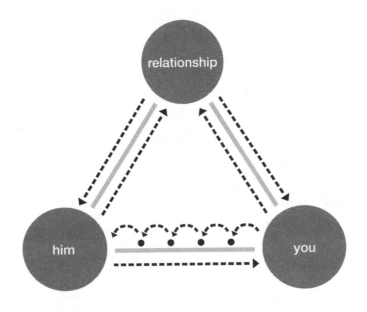

My family and I were spending a weekend on an island off the coast of Charleston with some other families, and my good friend and host for the weekend had an *aha!* moment regarding The Forty Beads Method as she approached us under the umbrellas after a long walk on the beach. She's a big-hearted, big-thinking woman and had been having some trouble getting next to the whole *sure thing* concept that's so crucial in The Method. Until she *got it.*

"I get it!" she said to me.

"You get what?" I said with a mouthful of beer and pistachios.

"I get why The Forty Beads Method works. It's because when you give your husband *what he loves* and you do that *out of love*, you can't help but *get love* in return."

That explains the whole love triangle, and I couldn't have said it better myself. It's all about the love—giving the love and getting the love in return. We Beaders? We Bead for love.

Part 3

Just the Facts, Ma'am

Just to be clear, I don't pretend to know or even really care to know all the reasons why sex is so hugely important to men. That would be a book unto itself. What follows are some interesting scientific tidbits, some nuggets I thought you might find interesting, that shed some light on the way men and women are just so different when it comes to sex. While the scientific material offered up here isn't exhaustive on the subject, I'm hoping it'll make some things you've always wondered about a little more clear, and at the very least, give you some interesting words like *medial preoptic nuclei* to toss out and impress your friends with at cocktail parties.

14

......

The Kinsey Studies and Steady Eddie

The Kinsey Studies were performed from 1938 until 1963 by Alfred Kinsey, a trailblazing Harvard-educated scientist who revolutionized the way the world understands sexual behavior. Before Kinsey came along, science hadn't really explored male and female sexuality, at least not above a whisper. Kinsey's findings were based on 18,600 face-to-face interviews, and although they've been quite controversial over the years, it's pretty hard to deny that his findings created the standards for sex research across the world. Kinsey and his staff had no problem digging around for the intimate details of their subjects' sex lives—like how often they had sex, what got them hot, and so on. And they didn't limit their explorative questioning to normal, run-of-the-mill sexual behavior. They covered the deviant shit, too. You'd think that most people would've shut old man Kinsey down when he got to the bit about bestiality. Gross. It turns out plenty of folks were all too happy to share their twisted fantasies and demented pasttimes in the name of science. And okay, a small portion of Kinsey's respondents were jailed criminals, but that just made them willing participants shirking laundry duty, not liars.

And if a Kinsey interviewer suspected any subject was bluffing, they cancelled the interview and tossed the data.

So the findings uncovered by the Kinsey studies are vast and varied and pretty informative. For one thing, their research found it to be true that we women can go the distance without getting any. We hit a dry spell of a few weeks, a few months, or even years, and we're okay with it. Well, I don't know about years, but the thing is, the studies found that as women, we're a lot less likely to go out and hunt down some action just because it's been a while. That's true, right? They also realized that we go through times when we're way into sex, and other times we just kind of forget about it. In other words, there's some ebb and flow when it comes to women's sexual desires.

Men aren't like that. Like I said before, they think they're dying a slow death if they're not getting laid regularly. The Kinsey studies found that there are no such irregularities in the consistency with which men engage in *some kind* of sexual activity. Are you catching my drift, ladies? How many times have you found your new soft, white hand towel tucked away in the laundry bin stiff as a board because he used it for his dream catcher? I know! It's totally gross, right? And sadly, no amount of bleach or fabric softener will restore your towel to its original splendor. Men are like Steady Eddie when it comes to sex. Even if they have to take matters into their own hands, it's gonna happen—one way or another. I don't know about you, but I'd rather have my man drop his desires into my Beadcatcher instead of an unsuspecting guest bathroom towel. I'm just saying.

15

......

Gentlemen, Start Your Engines

Another interesting thing that the Kinsey studies uncovered is that it just doesn't take all that much to get a guy's motor started. The sight of some hot strange woman walking down the street can give your man reason to readjust his package—especially if it's been a while. It's like some sort of chain reaction that happens in the brain. (More on that later.) And it's nothing personal to her or to you. It's just something that occurs. Maybe it's similar to how I react to a pan of chocolate chip cookies that just came out of the oven. Of course, I don't feel that in my genitals.

As women, we're just not like that. If we see some smokin' hot dude on the street, our reaction is not the same (at least for the most part). When we see a hot guy, the first thing we might do is start sizing him up as far as how he might fit into our life. Sure, he's hot, but I wonder what he *does*? Where is he *from*? Are those no-iron slacks? Eww!! It can be something as minor as a polyester blend (well, that's not really so minor) that will cause us to kick him to the curb even before we've exchanged sugar packets at the Starbucks counter. Men are different. If a girl looks really good to them, what do they do? They start picturing her on a bearskin rug. Naked. That's just how it is. And don't be fooled. Just because he's walking down the sidewalk in a chalk-striped navy suit, exhibiting an appropriate amount of decorum, that doesn't mean his inner cat-calling construction worker isn't raging within. Also, don't think that because your husband is out there in the world getting turned on by women all day long that he's some kind of pervert, because it's completely normal. More important, don't be thinking that it takes anything away from the super-fox that you are, because it doesn't.

A lot of folks didn't like Kinsey's findings, and since the research was done so long ago, they figured sexual behavior had probably changed a lot, especially after the sexual revolution and all. Turns out, later studies found much the same results: Men and women relate to sex the same way they always have—in very different ways. Apparently, we're just wired differently.

Bob Guccione found this out the hard way when he launched *Viva Magazine*, his 1970s *Penthouse* spinoff designed to tickle the female fancy. He assembled a fine team to head up the project, including then unknown British fashion editor Anna Wintour, among others, but the rag was doomed from the start. You see, Bob assumed that women would get off by looking at oiled-down beefcakes in *Viva* just like the dudes get all lathered up over the nudie shots in *Penthouse*. Bob was wrong. That kind of thing just doesn't do it for us. *Viva* launched in 1973 and shuttered its doors in 1980, and it was a big deal back then for a mag to fold like that. Bob's failed venture made it all too clear that women just don't really respond sexually to visual stimuli the way men do. Probably an expensive way to learn what doesn't do it for the ladies. Couldn't he have just run it by his wife at the time?

16

......

What a Large Medial

Preoptic You Have

So exactly how are we wired so differently? Well, while much of what goes on inside men's and women's brains when it comes to sex remains a mystery, science has figured out a few things and they have to do with some actual physical differences inside the male and female brains. For this to make sense, you first need to know that the part of the brain that's in charge of sexual arousal and desire is called the *diencephalon*, and it's right smack in the middle of the brain. For both men and women, this is the place in the brain where getting hot happens. Okay, so inside the diencephalon, there's this certain nucleus called the medial preoptic area, and scientists are pretty sure that for guys, this nucleus plays a crucial role in making them crave sex the way they do. And here's the interesting part: Turns out that this medial preoptic area in the male brain is like twice the size of that in the female brain. I know, what a shocker. And apparently you can tell just by eyeballing the thing. Just to make sure they got it right, scientists have done experiments with male monkeys where they yanked the medial preoptic right out of their brains and then watched to see what would happen. In his book *The Science of Happiness*, Stephan Klein went into some detail about what happened next, but basically, those little guys totally lost interest in sex. They did still enjoy a fair amount of masturbation (bet that was fun to watch), but they weren't the least bit interested in the cute little female monkeys anymore. So maybe this super-sized nucleus goes a long way toward explaining why guys are super-obsessed with sex. Roughly twice as big, roughly twice as into it—makes sense to me.

You've heard that the brain is the human body's biggest sex organ, right? Well, it's true. That's because, as humans, we apparently have a ton of brain mass that's specifically devoted to our genitals and their performance. In fact, a lot more than you'd think. And if the size of our vaginas and penises were in any way proportionally equal to their dedicated brain space, they'd be so big we'd have to wheel them around in wagons. Okay, maybe that's an exaggeration, but I think we'd have quite a bit of trouble walking upright.

17

······

Why Make-Up Sex Works

So we know that men and women need different stuff to get turned on, but another interesting thing going on is that men and women release two totally different types of hormones while they're having sex. Dudes release something called vasopressin, and we women release oxytocin. What I find particularly interesting is that both sexes have these two different hormones rushing through their brains during sex—right up until the crazy, fireworks, ending part. During orgasm is when men and women start pumping out the *same* sex hormone in their brains, oxytocin, known as the love hormone, which promotes emotional intimacy and has everything to do with making all of us feel really good. So it turns out there's a biological reason for why we feel so connected to each other after sex—it's all about oxytocin and sharing a moment on the same hormonal page. Isn't it interesting that, in the end, the dudes jump on over to our page? I'm just saying.

Stephan Klein talks about how sex is actually a well-designed "tool for peace"—an assertion bolstered by the scientific observations of sexy little bonobos monkeys. These monkeys are similar in size to chimpanzees and share more than 98% of our human DNA. (So, besides the extra hair, exactly *how* are we different?) So these guys just go ahead and *do it* whenever they're not getting along with each other. That's creative, isn't it? They don't call their monkey therapists, they don't sulk or suck their monkey thumbs—they just *get down*—right then and there—and then they move on. The bonobos have figured out that sex will squash any conflict they might have—whether it's a battle over the rightful owner of a pile of bananas or something more serious. And while it may not be pretty, it sure is quick and easy. Could it be *that* easy to clean-slate a situation in humans? It can be. Think about it. Ever come back together after a knock-down drag-out by way of some steamy make-up sex? That's because oxytocin rocks and bonobos monkeys are your kissing cousins. Now you know.

18

•••••

Sex and His Best Performance

There may even be a link for humans (especially the male humans) between sex and performance. We've talked about how the dudes spend a large portion of their time musing over all things sexual and that they spend even more time thinking about sex when they're not getting any. So it just makes sense to think that a guy who's sexually satisfied would be able to devote quite a bit more brain space to whatever it is he's trying to get done—whether it's winning a court case or playing cricket.

And speaking of playing cricket, according to the BBC, a coach for the Indian cricket team strongly advised his players to have sex the night before their big championship. I love it. I couldn't make this shit up if I tried. The coach floated some secret document among his players that extolled the benefits of sex before a game and even offered a little how-to on how those players less lucky in love could take matters into their own hands. "One option is to go solo whilst imagining you have a partner, or a few partners, who are as beautiful as you wish to imagine," the document suggested.

Classic. Did this dude really think this kind of delicious information wouldn't get leaked to the press? Maybe he didn't care, or maybe Coach needed to have a few screws professionally tightened. Anyway, this document explained that having sex would increase the players' testosterone levels, which would make them more aggressive and consequently help them to play better. While I agree that sex probably would make the cricketers play better, I'm thinking the reason for this would have more to do with them not being distracted by the heat emanating from their smoldering groins and less to do with some supposed testosterone spike. I mean, men aren't really aggressive after they've just had sex, are they? It's hard to be mean when you're sooo stinking happy.

Part 4

Sex as Commerce

Just the thought of coupling the words *sex* and *commerce* in any way might be a turn-off for you. I get it. It sounds bad and conjures up images of prostitution, pornography, and whatever else. But sex and money have a lot of similar attributes, and let's face it, both sex *and* money can make people do some pretty ridiculous things. The Forty Beads Method asks that you step outside the usual ways of thinking when it comes to pairing sex and commerce, and open yourself up to a whole different set of possibilities that exist when you marry sex and commerce (through the use of a token system) in an unconventional and totally positive way.

19
······
Beads as Currency

I was having a glass of wine with a friend when I first began writing this book, and she was a little skeptical.

"I don't know," she said. "It almost sounds like you're using beads as currency for sex."

"It's not almost like that," I said. "It's exactly like that. Where's the problem?"

Everybody knows that beads were used as currency back before anyone thought of pressing coins or printing money, but once I started dealing in Beads, I wanted to know more about their history. Turns out, beads were used in trading during the Neolithic period of human development, which fell at the tail end of the Stone Age, around 10,000 BC. That's a long time ago. I also learned that Venetian beads, like the ones my husband drops in my Beadcatcher, were used as currency during the 16th century throughout the Mediterranean, Europe, and Africa. It seems humans have used beads to get what they want, like, forever.

Taking up the long-abandoned token system and applying it to sex inside a marriage might seem like a crazy thing to do. Well, it's really not. As modern humans, we spend a lot of time in our heads—working out this and that, plotting our next move in business, or even planning our next meal. With all that stuff bumping around in our brains, wouldn't it be nice to move some of it out of our mental world and into our physical world—especially the important stuff that impacts our lives? The Forty Beads Method does that. In fact, it does even more, by taking sex out of the mind as a *possibility* and putting it out there in the physical world as a *definite*. That Bead in your Beadcatcher is a physical representation of your commitment to The Method and more important, your relationship. Using The Forty Beads Method separates sex from the things you *mean to do* in any 24-hour period and puts it with the items that you're *going to do*.

"Beading keeps me on track—it reminds me to do what makes my relationship great—which is, have sex with my husband. It's sort of like having a personal trainer. You keep your appointment, you work out and you feel so much better afterwards."

—AVA*

*JUST SO YOU KNOW, ALL NAMES HAVE BEEN CHANGED.

You *do* feel better about your relationship after sex. So why do we need reminding? We just do. But if you take up The Forty Beads Method, you never have to forget again.

20
......
Sex as a Commodity

My husband is a wealth advisor and has cautioned me against going into too much detail when discussing the ever volatile, pretty-stinking-complicated commodities market. But near as I can tell, sex in a marriage behaves a lot like a commodity, given that its fluctuations in value are based on supply and demand. When supplies of a certain commodity are tight, the value assigned to that commodity goes up and folks bust their asses trying to get more of that precious product. Have you ever seen those commodities traders in the pit of the Chicago Mercantile Exchange losing their shit trying to buy something before the price skyrockets? They're maniacs. I knew a guy who did that job for a while, and he had to smoke, like, a whole bag of weed every night just to get to sleep. I bet you know where I'm headed with this. When a man feels a sense of lack in the sex market of his marriage, when the supply just isn't there (and this is not a hard one for him to figure out), the value and attention he places on that scarce product goes up—as in, he can't think about much else except his squeezed-off access.

I've talked with friends and other Beaders about this phenomenon, and their experience of it is much like my own. When a guy feels like supplies are limited, he becomes consumed with the notion that he'll *never* get enough, which evolves into a self-fulfilling prophecy, because the more they act out of this fear of not getting enough, the less we're attracted to them, thus shutting down the supply even further. And I'm not even talking about asshole behavior here—more like the sad, manipulative behavior that just makes us roll our eyes and shake our heads. Don't they realize that desperation will never fall under the heading *Things That Turn Us On*? Are we bitches? I don't think so. What we want are positive, authentic actions born out of a genuine desire to connect. We respond favorably to that, right? We do not respond favorably to being poked at, wrangled, or guilted into having sex.

The good news is that unlike the world commodities market, which is subject to the effects of drought, miner strikes, and dwindling natural resources, the sex market inside your marriage expands and contracts at will. In other words, you make it rain. Here's what you have to decide: Will you (a) clamp down on the supply and create a frenzied, lack-driven obsession with regard to this commodity, or will you (b) open up the pipeline and enlist The Forty Beads Method to help you stabilize the ever volatile marital sex market, thereby restoring calm and goodwill to the home front?

Incidentally, sex in a marriage is *unlike* a commodity, however, in that as supply goes up (when it's happening regularly) a guy doesn't place any less value on it. He just gets happier. It doesn't take a degree in economics to figure that out. Additionally, an added value of using The Forty Beads Method is that when you make sex something that is readily available, your husband won't be so maniacally desperate for it. Nice, right? Just one of the many "Beadefits" (the benefits of using The Forty Beads Method) we'll discuss at length in Part 6.

21

The Oliver Twist Syndrome

Wouldn't you agree that your daily life is more enjoyable when you operate out of a sense of abundance rather than a sense of lack? It just feels better to believe that there's more than enough out there of whatever it is that you happen to need. As I mentioned earlier, men don't function well if they sense that there is a limited supply of sex available to them in their marriage. This brings us to the pitfalls of rationing sex in a marriage. If a man thinks that his chances of getting laid on any given night are between slim and none, it just makes him want that delicious fruit that much more.

When a man feels like he's getting rationed, he feels like Oliver Twist. ("Please, ma'am, may I have some more?") They hate this because it makes them feel weak, and that pisses them off. And never underestimate the reconnaissance skills of the sex-rationed male. He'll definitely be able to trace that pissed-off feeling back to you. Every time. Without exception. This is one reason why The Forty Beads Method works so well—it creates a sense of abundance around sex. Where rationing has a contracting effect on a relationship, Beading creates a majorly expansive experience.

22

......

Jackass and the Superfreak

When it comes to your husband's overall assessment of his personal sexual situation, it all boils down to quantity and frequency. How much and how often. Sure, quality factors in to a degree. But for the most part, your husband feels great about his sex life when he's getting plenty of sex on a regular basis. Here's the question: plenty, according to whom? That's a very subjective thing, right? What is a lot to one couple might be only marginally acceptable to another. And who *really* knows what's going on behind the curtain of anyone else's marriage, anyway? The question of whether we're dealing in fact or fiction doesn't stop us (men *and* women) from discussing and speculating about the sex habits of other people.

As women, if we're curious, our interest is usually voyeuristic in nature: "I didn't know she was into *that*! I *so* would not go there with him!" When guys talk about their sex lives with other men, they do so only to figure out how their own sexual situation stacks up against the rest. These are conversations that men walk away from striding a little taller in their shoes or feeling cut off at the knees. Why do they do this to themselves? I don't know, except that every guy must hold out hope that at some point he'll be the one who's had the most sex, the one left holding the long end of the stick, comparatively speaking. It always goes back to the stick, doesn't it? Length, notches—whatever.

I'm not saying that guys powwow about their sex lives every time they go out for beers, but it does happen. And chances are, your husband has at least one guy in his life, either an office mate, a fishing buddy or maybe a golfing partner, who brags about how much his wife puts out. It could even be a guy your husband doesn't know all that well, who may or may not be telling the truth, but guess what? It doesn't matter. Your husband will believe him because what this jackass is bragging about actually confirms his worst suspicion: "Dammit! I knew it! *Everybody* gets it more than I do." It doesn't take a dream weaver to picture how the scene plays out:

Your husband's getting drinks after work with some colleagues, and after they're good and lubed up, Jack (we'll call Jackass by his nickname, Jack) leans in to confide in his closest work buds that his wife Carol just can't get enough. Maybe he even takes it so far as to pretend like it's become some kind of burden for him, his cross to bear, since she makes him do it *all the time*. Uh huh. He might even cite some strange and seedy places they've done it, just to beef up the story. As Rick James would have said: She's a superfreak. Or at least that's what Jack would have your husband believe. And maybe she is. It really doesn't matter, but one thing's for sure: While your husband and his friends are rapt in this fantastically sexy tale, he's doing a little math in his head, and it goes something like this:

When's the last time we did it? I know it had to be three weeks ago (although it could have been last week and he selectively forgot that time). *Well, one thing's for sure—I'm not getting it like Jack does. This is bullshit. She is such a bitch. I shouldn't say that. I love my wife. Jack's wife doesn't look like the type, but you never know. My life is shit.*

This information has left an indelible impression in the far reaches of your husband's brain. This is information he will never forget. It may get mangled and, no doubt, exaggerated over the years, but I promise you he will never lose track of it and will refer back to it during the leaner sexual times of your relationship, and it will piss him off. Men love sex, and they hate thinking that they're getting less of it than other guys. It's like they're in some kind of competition, right? I'm not saying it's right, I'm just saying that's how it is.

Part 5

Getting Your Bead On

THE FORTY BEADS CREED

Important Rules of Beading

RULE #1
Be Generous with the Number of Beads
You Gift Him: Go for 40

Remember, you're creating a sense of abundance around
what he loves most in this world.

RULE #2
Take Charge

Be assertive when gifting the Beads—they love that.

RULE #3
Tend to Your Beadcatcher

Keep a watchful eye—let no Bead go unacknowledged.

RULE #4
Preserve the Integrity of Your Beads

Use your advanced Beading moves to maintain forward
motion in your Beading Practice.

RULE #5
Redeem Every Bead in a Timely Fashion
Honor the 24-hour Bead redemption window.

RULE #6
Honor Every Bead
Don't stop to consider the merit of individual Beads.

RULE #7
Don't Get Cocky
Never abandon the Bead—even when you *know*
you're a Beading expert.

RULE #8
Have Fun with Your Beading Adventure
Enjoy the fun, easy flow The Forty Beads Method
brings to your marriage.

RULE #9
Beader's Choice: Adopting a Green Bead Policy
If you're having fun, recycle your Beads.

We've studied sex from lots of angles, and now we're finally at the hands-on part. What follows is the how-to portion of the book, which gives you every detail about *what* to do, what you definitely *don't* want to do, and how to wriggle your way out of any unintended Beading jams. If there's something I failed to cover, a snag or a fine point you'd like me to explain more, just Beadmail me at carolyn@fortybeads.com and we'll talk it through. The Method is pretty straightforward, but you know how they say that the devil hangs out in the details? That's because it's true. Sometimes the easiest things are the ones I screw up the fastest. And trust me when I tell you, some really intelligent couples have gotten things really wrong right from the start. So we'll go through it bit by bit, and as we do, remember, The Forty Beads Method is for you (and your relationship and your husband).

One very important thing: Please read *all* of Part 5—the whole thing—as well as spend some time *getting good* with The Forty Beads Creed printed here *before* beginning your Beading adventure. I know that sounds anal, but after working with so many Beaders, I've realized that doing this will help ensure that your Beading practice starts off on the right foot. So read The Forty Beads Creed, maybe sleep on it or even sleep with it under your pillow. It doesn't matter—just do whatever it takes to *internalize* The Creed, so that you're ready to honor it. Different Beaders do different things to prepare themselves for their Beading practice. One semi-reluctant Beader found that spending time with the Beads themselves helped her wrap her mind around the process she was getting ready to commit to.

"I carried those Beads around in my purse for three weeks before I gave them to my husband on the night of our anniversary. I was excited to get started, but also had some fear and guilt around sex and the small amount we'd had of it in recent years. As I carried around those Beads, I started constructing this bridge in my mind. I processed all my emotions around giving him the Beads—fear, anxiety, resentment, but in the end, I realized what I really wanted was love—to give it and receive it. So after some Bead handling and soul searching, I gave him the Beads with no reservations and it was a moment I will never forget. As we sat cross-legged on the bed, I handed him the sack of Beads and said, 'I want these Beads to be my bridge back to you.' That was my intention and that's exactly what the Beads have been—a bridge that re-connected us to each other."

—EMILY

That is one brilliant Beader. The bridge metaphor kills me. Before we get down to the nuts and bolts of The Forty Beads Method, I'd like you to keep in mind that every new Beader brings two sexual stories to her Beading practice: her own personal sexual story and the sexual story of her marriage. Some of these stories carry pain, guilt, anxiety, or anger. That's okay. We all have our stories. And we've all done the best we could with the information and experiences we've had up to this point, right? Even if you have a history that includes sexual abuse, promiscuity, or anything else that could've lacquered your sexual experiences with shame or guilt, The Forty Beads Method might show you a new way to experience your sexuality that's easeful and fun. I've been so delighted to hear that The Method has been helpful to lots of women in healing their scarred sexual histories.

If sex has been a sticking point for you in your marriage, it is my greatest hope that The Forty Beads Method will give you the tools you need to create a turning-point moment in the story of your marriage and your life.

23

......

The Gift That Keeps On Giving

 THE FORTY BEADS CREED :: RULE #1

Be Generous with the Number of Beads You Gift Him: Go for 40

Remember, you're creating a sense of abundance around what he loves most in this world.

The Forty Beads Method evolved from a gift that I gave my husband. So as you put The Method into action, remember that the Beads really are a gift—a gift unlike any you've given before. (You're probably pretty clear on that point, right?) And the Beads really are the gift that keeps on giving—and not just to him, but to you, and most important, to your marriage. With that in mind, you'll want to present the Beads as the super-fine gift that they are. There's nothing run-of-the-mill about this gift, so you don't want to just slap it in front of him like the tie he got for Christmas last year.

Women have found all sorts of creative ways to present the gift of the Beads. One woman sewed her own velvet patchwork pouch for the Beads, found a little hand-carved wooden bowl for her Beadcatcher, and wrapped it all up in a box with a satin bow.

Another woman fashioned a gift basket with fun little goodies she knew he'd love and tucked the Beads in a heart-shaped box inside the basket. I love these creative approaches, but me, I'm not so crafty. So for other artistically challenged women like myself and also for those interested in one-stop shopping, I put together The Forty Beads Gift. You can find it on the website www.fortybeads.com, and it has everything you'll need to kick off your Beading practice—all neatly packaged in a handsome gift box ready to be given.

Elements You'll Need for The Forty Beads Gift
- one small bowl (about 3½ inches in diameter maybe 1½ inches deep)
- 40 Beads (in some sort of pouch or bag that keeps them contained)
- 3 Nudge Cards (small cards that say "Bead Me" on them—totally optional)

Whether you make it yourself or purchase The Forty Beads Gift online, what you're first going to need is a little bowl about the size of a soy sauce dish, but with taller sides. (That's your Beadcatcher.) When you put The Forty Beads Method into action, you will place that Beadcatcher on your bedside table or some other place where you don't have to go out of your way to see it. Important: It needs to be placed in *your* space—so that he is approaching *your* shelf in the closet or the top of *your* dresser to drop a Bead. Don't let your Beadcatcher hang out next to his Bead stash—that could create a sense that he's just Beading with himself, and that's no fun. Placement of your Beadcatcher is crucial. It needs to be in a place where you'll definitely notice when a Bead has been dropped—if you have to remember to go and check it, you might forget, and that's no good. Your Beadcatcher should be out of reach of small hands (little girls love to steal a lone Bead in a bowl—not helpful!) and out of eyesight of prying teenagers (you might choose to tell your teen all about your Beading practice—but it should be *your* choice—not under duress when barraged with questions). Once you begin your Beading practice, you'll see that your Beadcatcher becomes your little altar of love. One Beading couple calls it their nest, which I think is perfect.

Next, you'll need some Beads. You could cut up an old necklace you don't like anymore or head over to your local hippie bead store. As a practical matter, you don't want to use some tiny bead that he can't easily pick up with his thumb and forefinger. Make it a colorful bead (the Beads in The Forty Beads Gift are a sexy, crimson red color) and a meaty bead (12 mm is good)—one he could actually find if he dropped it, because at some point he will. And let me tell you, when he does, he's not going to rest until he finds it. One Beader gave her husband the Beads on a weekend away from the kids, and when they got home, he couldn't find them and came to her in a panic. He found his Beads, but he nearly had a coronary before he did. Make it easy for him to keep his Beads together by giving him something to put them in. The Forty Beads Gift has a little leather pouch (pigskin, actually—like a football!) that guys can pull tight and tuck into their sock drawer. Anything that closes will do.

Why 40 Beads? As you know, I gave my husband 40 for his 40th birthday, and I think part of why The Method works so well is because 40 *feels* like a lot. (That's because it *is* a lot.) It felt heavy in the envelope, and there was no way to count the Beads without lining them up across the hotel room floor. (He didn't do that.) He didn't feel the need to count them, because he knew for sure that I'd given him way more Beads than he could use up in a single week or even one steamy month. That's important. We're going for life-changing impact here, and you're not going to get that if he can count his Beads just by eyeballing them.

When I picked the number 40, I had no idea how significant, symbolically speaking, it really is. As an elevation of the number four, 40 symbolizes wholeness and totality. The Roman quarantine kept ships isolated for 40 days. Temples in Persia and those of the Druids had 40 pillars. There are 40 days in Lent, from Christ's 40 days in the wilderness. In the Old Testament, it was 40 years that the Jews wandered in the desert before reaching the Promised Land. It rained for 40 days and 40 nights when God wanted to give the earth a good hosing down. In the Islamic religion, Mohammed received his call when he was 40 years old, and also, according to Islam, 40 is the number of reconciliation and return to the principle.

I especially like this bit about reconciliation, since The Forty Beads Method is really good at bringing couples back together—both physically and emotionally. And returning to the principle? That's got to mean getting back to the basics, and The Forty Beads Method is all about that. The Method provides a steady reminder that sex is a simple, basic, and important part of a healthy marriage. In addition, I just found out that after a man gets a vasectomy he's got to ejaculate 40(!) times before he starts shooting blanks. That was some well-timed, useful information I was happy to run across. So when it comes to numbers, 40 is a really good one—not just for a 40th birthday, but any old time.

So 40 is the number of Beads used in The Method because it feels like a generous amount. And being generous with the number of Beads you give him is important, because it's all about creating that sense of abundance, which will play an important role in the big shift that happens in your relationship. You might just have to take my word on this, but being big-hearted from the start and going for 40 will *definitely* serve you well—the bounty comes right back to you. And I don't mean to be a bitch (really, I don't), but if you're only comfortable with handing over a small handful of Beads (like, say, ten) then you're just not ready for The Forty Beads Method. That's okay. Hold onto the book, and maybe you'll pull it out again when you're really needing some change and feel ready to step up to the plate. Like most things in life, The Forty Beads Method is all about timing, and when it feels right for you, you'll know. Not sure if you're ready? Check out the New Beader's Checklist. (See below.)

The New Beader's Checklist

Here are a few questions to help you decide if The Forty Beads Method is right for you. If you answer *yes* to most of the following questions, then you're ready to begin Beading.

1. Do you love your husband?
2. Do you want to stay married to him?
3. Do you have this sneaking suspicion that your relationship has the potential to be better than it is?
4. Do you ever experience any confusion, anger, guilt, or stress associated with sex in your marriage?
5. Are you interested in making your relationship the best (happiest, most easeful, most fun) it can be?
6. Are you willing to incorporate changes in order to develop a better relationship?
7. Are you interested in making sex in your marriage something that you *want* to do instead of something you feel like you *should* do?
8. Do you find value in feeling emotionally connected to your husband?

Of course, if you feel like trumping me, go ahead. My mom did. She gave my dad 72 Beads for his birthday this year. So go ahead. Go for 40 (or more!). When you see what happens to your relationship, you'll be glad you were so generous.

The last element of The Forty Beads Gift is the Nudge Card. In the gift I designed, there are three small, kind of elegant little cards that simply say, "Bead Me." Of course, you could make a Nudge Card out of a sticky note as well. The Nudge Cards give a woman a way (if she so chooses) to put it out there that she'd like a Bead—just by dropping a card on his dresser. While I've never personally had need for a Nudge Card, there are situations where women have found them to come in handy.

First of all, I can't tell you how many men, after hearing all about how their lives are about to change with The Forty Beads Method, circle back around to their wives and say, "But I want *you* to Bead *me* too!" You know what? Good for them for thinking that they'd get Beaded, but we're working off of the *more active* male sex drive here, which typically initiates more than enough sex for all involved. Bottom line: The Beads just go the one way. He holds the Beads. He drops the Bead. The two of you redeem the Bead together. Beads traveling in different directions would lead to confusion and disappointment. If we women got a bunch of Beads, months would pass and we'd likely still have a bunch of Beads—and one depressed dude. But for those of you interested in becoming more involved in the dropping of the Beads, the Nudge Cards work great.

Nudge Cards are also useful when it's the husband with the low libido. Some women have used The Forty Beads Method to pull their husbands out of their sexual malaise—we'll talk more about this in Chapter 28, Opening Pandora's Box. Although it's way more common for the woman to have the lower sex drive, it really does happen sometimes that it's the guy who's just not feeling it. Nudge Cards definitely come in handy when this is the case.

One last thing about the Nudge Cards: You know if you need them, and if you don't, then just forget about them. They're totally optional, really effective if you do need them, and of course, completely recyclable. And a word to the wise: If you buy The Forty Beads Gift and don't intend to use the Nudge Cards, be sure and snatch them out of the box before you gift the Beads—no point in needlessly confusing his excellent situation.

Characteristics of the Beads

There are some important things you need to know about the Beads before you toss them:

One Equals One. Although it may be obvious, I just want to be clear that each Bead is good for one roll in the hay.

Beads Don't Expire. It wouldn't be prudent to issue a date of expiration for your Beads. It could lead to needless squandering of the Beads if your husband is under the impression that they might go bad, especially if he's one of those guys who can't stand to see something go to waste. You know the type—they'll stand at the fridge and drink all the milk before you go on vacation since it would be spoiled when you got home. He'll breathe a sigh of relief when he understands that his Beads don't lose their value over time.

Beads Are Non-Transferrable. Maybe it goes without saying, but I'll still just put it out there that the Beads are redeemable only between you and your husband. For example, don't pull them out when you're hosting a dinner party and pass a few under the table to your husband's friend you've always had a crush on—that'd be begging for trouble.

24

······

The Great Bead Toss

THE FORTY BEADS CREED :: RULE #2

Take Charge

Be assertive when gifting the Beads—they love that.

From the start, keep in mind is that this is *your* Beading adventure. I'll give you the guidelines, but how you decide to kick off your Beading practice is totally up to you—go low-key or totally over-the-top with it—your choice. Some women like to gift the Beads on a birthday, anniversary, Father's Day, or Valentine's Day, but often that's not convenient, so really, any time will do.

If you feel like it, get creative when gifting the Beads. This beginning bit, when he's first hearing about how his life is about to change, is key because it sets the tone for your Beading adventure. And while it's pretty simple, it's also important to follow the details carefully. Like I said before, plenty of really smart people have screwed it up right out of the gate.

Bead Gifting Examples

Here are some fun examples of creative Bead gifting I've gotten from fellow Beaders. (By the way, I'd love to hear your story, too. Go to www.fortybeads.com and tell me all about it.)

- One woman sneaked into her husband's office when he was at lunch one day and left the Beads on his desk with a note that said, "Bring these home tonight!" Adds an element of intrigue, don't you think?

- While staying at a hotel overnight with her husband, one woman tipped room service a little extra to bring in the Beads under a silver dome. Ooh, la la—dessert, anyone?

- One unsuspecting husband found a sack of Beads tucked inside his golf bag—in the driver head cover! You've got to love the double meaning on that one.

Don't be tentative when gifting the Beads. This is all about you taking the bull by the horns; it's not about you coming to him and saying, "Should we try this?" No. It's about you looking him in the eye and saying, "Here's what we're going to do," and him looking really confused and then delighted. Here's what one Beader had to say about her husband's reaction to the Beads:

"We were driving to a weekend away with some other couples. As we got on the highway, I gave him the Beads and told him what they were for. He said, 'What? There's no way. You won't do it!' I was patient and circled back, insisting on my commitment, and told him, 'Yes. This is the new deal. Period.' He was silent for about a mile and then got the silliest perma-grin on his face that lasted for the rest of the hour-and-a-half car ride. That grin was interrupted only by spontaneous bouts of giddy laughter. I was like, 'Oh my god, you're a freak!' He said, 'Maybe, but I'm the happiest freakin' man alive!' "

—ANNA

The Sequence of Events

(Remember to read *all* of this section, Getting Your Bead On, and spend some time with The Forty Beads Creed, *before* putting your Beads in motion!)

1. Gift him the Beads. Remember to gift the Beads when you're ready to begin Beading—not weeks before. That's just mean.

2. Explain that each Bead is good for one roll in the hay.

3. Show him to your Beadcatcher, where he will drop his Beads—one at a time. Explain to him that's how you'll know he's ready.

4. Tell him about the 24-hour redemption window. (More information on that follows.)

5. Reiterate to him that, yes, you're serious, and that Beading begins when he drops the first Bead.

Those five steps make up the better part of his introduction to the Beading process, but of course, he'll want to know more, so you can tell him all about the characteristics of the Beads from the previous chapter and the advanced Beading maneuvers explained in chapters that follow.

You might want to pay particular attention to the look on his face when you get to the bit about the redemption process. He may be skeptical. That's okay. The Forty Beads Method is truly something that has to be experienced firsthand to be believed. He might think you'll flake out on him and won't keep it up. Be committed. One Beader turned her husband's initial skepticism into her personal, voice-in-the-head cheering section:

"I still sometimes think he's waiting for me to drop the whole Beading process because he can't believe that I'll keep it up. That just spurs me on—I'll show him!"

—MARTHA

The Forty Beads Method works, but only if you work it. I mean, you wouldn't really expect to become a skinny bitch just by reading the *Skinny Bitch* book, would you? You have to actually *do* something to create the change you want in your life—whether it's dropping 20 or getting the rock-solid, envy-worthy relationship you so clearly deserve.

Here's your first Beading mantra:

 BEADING MANTRA #1

I Work the Beads and the Beads Work for Me

Repeat it when you're feeling discouraged, and it'll be like a rock-climbing crampon to help you re-establish secure footing.

Be patient with the guy if he's skeptical, and just steadily work The Method. You've got to remember, he's used to thinking *about* the box, not outside of it, and this is a pretty radical concept. He'll probably approach you later with a set of questions he didn't think of when you first tossed him the sack of Beads. Go with it. That's part of the fun.

25

······

The Bead Drop and the

Redemption Process

 THE FORTY BEADS CREED :: RULE #3

Tend to Your Beadcatcher

Keep a watchful eye—let no Bead go unacknowledged.

Let's look at how this whole thing is going play out. Just *how* the Bead gets dropped depends on the dude, the day, and his particular mood at that moment. Some guys like to be real obvious and will approach your Beadcatcher with the whole *I am such a stud* swagger while you're reading in bed. The swagger is usually joined by a confident grin (you know the one) and an extra loud "plink" in your Beadcatcher. Others enjoy treating the Bead drop like it's some kind of clandestine mission and approach your Beadcatcher for deposit only when they're sure no one's looking. A little 007 action—that's cool. What's pretty universal is that men like to have fun with their Bead dropping. What's also really common is that we find that pretty cute. That little "plink" sound when the Bead hits the Beadcatcher? One husband called that "the most beautiful sound in the world," and I have to agree with him.

Now on to what you're most concerned with—the redemption of the Bead. We're all reasonable, practical people, right? And we're all busy as hell. So it makes sense that there needs to be a buffer of time between the Bead drop and the actual redemption of that Bead. That's really the only way to work The Method. So here it is: You should be prepared to redeem the Bead sometime in the following 24 hours after it's dropped into your Beadcatcher. This isn't a sex-on-demand sort of thing, it's more like a sex-as-soon-as-is-reasonably-possible kind of thing. A lot of women say that this buffer of time is what they like most about using The Method—it's what makes the sexual exchange more doable for them. I will say that if he drops a Bead and you feel like dropping into the sack immediately, you can do that, but don't be telling him that's how The Method works. If you have that kind of flexibility, that's great, but I would caution against an immediate Bead redemption, *especially* in the beginning, because it sets a bad precedent.

The Forty Beads Method is about promoting consistency in your sex life, and chances are, you're not going to be willing to strip down immediately every time a Bead gets dropped. Most important, you wouldn't get the benefit of the anticipation—that delicious and very important slice of the Beading pie. It's that promise of getting it on that he holds in his heart and mind that permeates the space between you two and lifts the relationship to higher ground. Some scientists say that it's actually the *anticipation* of sex that men enjoy more than the actual deed itself. Most men I know would disagree, but the point is, the "looking forward to it" is a lot of why The Forty Beads Method rocks a marriage. And remember in the beginning of the book when we talked about how often a man thinks about sex? Well, since he's going to be thinking about it all day long anyway, he might as well be anticipating having sex with *you*, right?

The way of the Bead goes something like this:

1. He feels that twitch or that itch or whatever it is and scoops up a Bead.
2. He drops that Bead in your Beadcatcher, conveniently placed on your bedside table or some other easy-to-see spot.
3. He feels a rush of sexual anticipation, pure joy, and gratitude in the assurance that his wife is a sure thing.
4. He gives you the best version of himself. In other words, he behaves in all the ways he knows you like.
5. You spy the Bead in your Beadcatcher and acknowledge it by going to him and saying something like, "Hey, I see you've Beaded me. Thanks!"
6. You join him in thinking about when you two will get it on in the coming 24 hours, which you're happy to do because you're feeling connected to him since he's being so great.
7. You two hit the sheets.
8. You remove the Bead from your Beadcatcher and tuck it away with the other redeemed Beads in your underwear drawer or secret recycling Bead bin. (We'll talk about recycling Beads—totally up to you—later.)

Make sure he tucks his Beads away some place safe. One Beader came into her bedroom to find her four-year-old daughter attempting to string up her daddy's Beads into a necklace for mommy. Those aren't just any old Beads—Daddy's got plans for those Beads, so he should make sure they're out of the reach of tiny hands.

Little questions from curious little ones: One Beader said that her son asked what that Bead was for in that bowl. Quick thinker that she is, she explained that those are Daddy's idea Beads. Whenever he has a good idea, he puts a Bead in the bowl. Her answer was so boring, she (thankfully) never got asked again.

An interesting thing that happens once you start Beading is that you'll find yourself going out of your way to check and see if there's a Bead in your Beadcatcher. Who'd have thought you'd be looking for it, right?

"I reminded my husband about his Beads this morning! I was actually bummed not to have a Bead in my Beadcatcher. Me, bummed—that's huge!"

—OLIVIA

It's fun to glance at your Beadcatcher—just to see—but also important for practical planning purposes. And that's part of the deal because you're going to want to stay on top of your Beading practice. Bead acknowledgment is an important part of the Beading process, so don't get caught falling asleep at the wheel. You may experience a little wave of excitement when you notice that a Bead has been dropped, and maybe a little tinge of disappointment when he hasn't dropped a Bead for a while. That's all part of the process and a lot of what makes The Method so much fun. You'll likely be surprised by what seeing a Bead in your Beadcatcher stirs up for you.

So once you begin Beading, there's a nice layer of anticipation mixed with creativity (as you design your moment) that gets added to your relationship. If you have small children, you might have to call upon that creativity more often than not in securing your moment, but with a little effort, it'll unfold nicely. One Beading couple simply announces to their little ones: "Daddy and I are going to have a meeting, and we'll be with you when the meeting is over." Then they lock the bedroom door. The kids think nothing of it, and so far, they've never asked why Mommy has that dewy glow after a meeting.

Another thing that happens as a result of the Beading process is that the stress-inducing, not-so-great layers associated with sex in your relationship just fall away. For one thing, you get to skip the brain-teasing frustration of trying to figure out when your husband is ready for some action and determining if he's about to blow his top because he thinks it's been way too long.

"Once I started Beading, I felt so relieved. I didn't realize how much pressure it was for me to read his mind and try to be on the same page with him when I just wasn't. Once I saw the Bead in the bowl it sort of triggered my mind and I started thinking more about us and not about everything else that goes on around us. The Bead takes the sexual conjecture out of our marriage."

—SARAH

Once you wrap your head around the idea that sex is a large part of how he expresses and grows his love for you, the Bead begins to symbolize just that—his love/adoration for you.

"Seeing a Bead in my Beadcatcher always makes me smile. I love knowing that hubby wants me. I mean, I've always *known* he wanted me, but that Bead is actual proof."

—ASHLEY

You'll start to put it together that a Bead drop is an undeniable indication that your husband's been thinking about you. That feels good, right? It's all about the love. And don't you just *love* love? When you get right down to it, it's really all there is.

26

......

Beading Details and

Advanced Moves

Preserve the Integrity of Your Beads

Use your advanced Beading moves to maintain forward motion in your Beading Practice.

I am not a detail person. I prefer wide swaths and broad strokes, but there are certain intricacies involved in the Beading process that just have to be addressed. So forgive me for getting all technically anal, but as your fairy Bead mother it is my job to guide you in creating the most snafu-free Beading experience possible.

From the moment you embark on your Beading adventure, you are charged with preserving the integrity of the Beads. This is important because, as I've mentioned, during the Beading process, the Beads begin to symbolize a lot of good things about your relationship. You want to protect that, right? That's why it's important for you to observe certain parameters that will ensure that your Beads maintain their value once they're put into action.

What follows are some specific do's and don'ts as well as ways to wriggle your way out of some common Beading jams.

THE FORTY BEADS CREED :: RULE #5
Redeem Every Bead in a Timely Fashion.
Honor the 24-hour Bead redemption window.

⊛ DON'T LET THE BEAD LANGUISH

The effectiveness of The Forty Beads Method rests on the assurance that each Bead that's dropped will be redeemed in a timely fashion. The languishing Bead is a lonely, unredeemed Bead that's left to hang out in its Beadcatcher way past its redemptive due date, and let me tell you, you're going want to avoid that. You see, each little Bead holds all this intention and positive energy at the moment that it drops, but if it gets *put on hold* (as in, it's still there after the 24-hour window has passed), its energy is diminished. This could happen, say, if your man dropped a Bead on his way out the door for a week-long business trip. That's no good. You would walk past your Beadcatcher every day while he's gone, and you might start to feel like you're not holding up your end of the deal, when that's not the case at all.

Beading is about keeping things fresh and moving forward in your relationship, and redeeming a fresh Bead is a lot more fun and effective than dealing with one that's been kept in a holding pattern. This is true with most things. Would you rather spend

200 calories on a Krispy Kreme doughnut you found in a gas station or on a just-glazed hot one? No contest. So there should always be some time stretched out in front of a Bead drop, otherwise it should just stay in his stash.

Make it a rule that if that 24-hour redemption window following the Bead drop is not available (due to one of you going out of town or something) he should wait to drop the Bead until that window is there. Sometimes he might have to use a little finesse when dropping the Bead, but that's nothing considering the lengths he used to go to creating the whole seduction routine, right? Trust me, he won't mind—it's worth it to keep the Beads in play. So you think that rule might create its own different set of problems? I've got you covered—keep reading.

⊛ BOUNCING A BEAD

There will be those rare cases when a Bead has dropped and redemption in a timely fashion is impossible—due to a partner's unexpected absence, an illness, or an injury. That's when you have to bounce the Bead so the Bead isn't left to languish. A "Bead bounce" is when you toss the Bead back into his Bead stash. It's sort of like restarting your computer—you only want to do it when it's absolutely necessary, because if you do it too much, the thing might start breaking down. Just like your computer, your Beading practice would surely break down if you made a habit of bouncing Beads. So while you want to guard against excessive bouncing, the necessary Bead bounce shouldn't have any negative connotation, because it's done in order to *preserve the integrity of the Beads.* Important: When you have to bounce a Bead, you'll want to talk to him about what you're doing and why. For example, say you wake up with a nasty cold or the flu and you realize that he Beaded you the night before. That Bead has to get bounced because the chance of you getting to that Bead in the next 24 hours? Not likely. So you might say something like:

"Hey, I see you dropped a Bead last night and I know you don't want a piece of this action, so I'm just gonna to toss it back into your stash and let you know when I'm feeling better, 'kay?"

He should be cool with that—it shows your commitment to the process, and your commitment is the whole reason why The Forty Beads Method is so effective.

🏵 BEADING BY PROXY

The Forty Beads Method is about moving your sex life forward, not putting it in a holding pattern. I really don't think your man would find it amusing if, when he got home from a weeklong business trip, you told him to drop a Bead and you'd be with him in the next 24 hours. That's where Beading by proxy comes in, and it's sort of like riding a fake Vespa—not as good as the real thing, but it'll get you where you need to be. Beading by proxy is when he calls or emails or texts you and asks you to slip a Bead into your Beadcatcher on his behalf. You'll have to let him know about this technical Beading move at some point. For example, just as he's leaving for a business trip, you could fill him in. That's sexy. It's totally fun and opens an opportunity for that secret conversation between the two of you, which builds the anticipation that we all love. He'll board that airplane with a swing in his step and a goofy grin on his face, just thinking about you and your sexy offer.

Important: What's not allowed is *virtual* Beading. He can't just email or text you and say, "I'm Beading you." No, he's not. He's just being lazy, and that doesn't work. The Bead has to physically make it to the Beadcatcher for the magic to happen. So Beading by proxy is cool. Virtual Beading—not cool.

THE FORTY BEADS CREED :: RULE #6
Honor Every Bead
Don't stop to consider the merit of individual Beads.

✪ SUSPEND JUDGMENT

Suspending judgment refers to probably the stickiest rule in the whole Forty Beads Creed, and so it deserves a little extra time. There may be times when you'll be tempted to question the worthiness of a certain Bead that's been dropped. You might think that in light of some recent slack-ass or insensitive behavior that he doesn't really *deserve* that Bead redemption. You have to make a conscious choice *not* to go there in your mind. While this is the most challenging part of using The Forty Beads Method, it's also the most crucial piece to internalize and follow with determination.

I Bead for Love

Remember that when you redeem a Bead (especially when you don't feel like it) you are choosing love, and by choosing love, that is exactly what you'll get in return. Don't you love that?

Remember that the most important element, the foundation upon which the whole Forty Beads Method rests, is the fact that you're a sure thing, and with the exception of some serious asshole behavior (you know what that looks like), that's exactly what you are. Part of what makes this Method so effective is that it helps you to focus on the "big picture" of your marriage, rather than the annoying minutiae. When you decide to use The Forty Beads Method, you're also deciding that you want to *rise above* the petty grievances that routinely creep into a marriage instead of getting dragged down by them. It's about moving the relationship forward, and experiencing The Method firsthand is really the only way to understand how it works. So for now, maybe you'll just take my word for it that you can't question the worthiness of each Bead that's dropped, because keeping a "big picture" approach in your Beading practice is really, *really* crucial.

By the way, I am the master of making mountains out of molehills. I know how easy (and in a sick way, how fun) it can be to obsess over some little something. I can take one of my husband's slightly insensitive remarks, trace its origin back to his childhood, gather evidence to support my theory and cite examples of other tactless remarks made throughout the course of our marriage—all to prove my point at that moment that he just doesn't appreciate me enough. I did this plenty until I realized how pointless it was. Sure, it's important to clear the air when a thoughtless comment is made, but it's been my experience that focusing on the stuff you don't want only gets you more of that stuff you don't want.

Over the course of using The Forty Beads Method, I've found that the benefits I get from using The Method are so much more valuable to me than the twisted joy of chewing on some bullshit remark. So even when he's done something stupid or said something that pissed me off, I don't use it as an excuse to sabotage our Beading practice. The Forty Beads Method can't put an end to stupid things that men do (P.S. We do a lot of stupid things, too), but it *can* make it easier to move past them in a timely manner. The committed Beader repeatedly decides to take the high road and move on to a better emotional place instead of hanging out in Pissedville. And by now, you've figured me out enough to know that I've spent many a night there. I hate it in Pissedville, and I want to spend as little time there as possible. It's lonely and uncomfortable, and it's pretty much impossible to get a good night's sleep when you're punching your pillow. So you can choose anger and opposition, or you can choose love. Love feels better, don't you think? And anyway, do you really have a good reason for postponing your own joy? This might be another good time to remind you that The Forty Beads Method is for you (and him, and your relationship).

So you'll choose love, and it's in that moment when you push on through and stay the course of the Beading way, that you pave (or should I say Bead) a path to the next level of goodness in your relationship.

"Redeeming a Bead when you're irritated with your husband or just tired is like holding a long pose in yoga. You feel the burn and you think there's no way you're going to go through with it, but you're committed to The Method and so you do. And just like that, you've made it through and you both feel great—about each other—and once again all is right in your married world."

—BROOKE

Remember that every choice we make and every action we take either brings us closer to or pulls us further from the love we want.

✿ TURTLING YOUR BEADCATCHER

It happens. Fundamentally good guys with well-established Beading practices sometimes go off the reservation with some crazy-bullshit-lunatic behavior and render themselves unBeadable. Temporarily. I must emphasize that this kind of behavioral exhibition should be pretty rare. That's because, wouldn't a guy who consistently demonstrates asshole behavior, in fact, *be* an asshole? If that's the case, he would be unBeadable from the start—remember, assholes don't get to Bead. So in the rare event that your man loses his shit with some truly shameful, inglorious behavior (and I'm trusting you to be able to distinguish that from run-of-the-mill irritating behavior), that probably means it's time to turtle your Beadcatcher. Turtling is a simple act of turning your Beadcatcher upside down on the table and thereby sending a clear message that your sure-thing status has been suspended.

How long should he stay in Beading purgatory? Well, it definitely depends on the offense, but generally speaking, three days should be enough. In our first year of Beading, my husband turtled his Beadcatcher just the one time. It was around Christmas, and we were discussing (arguing) about holiday plans when his temper flared in my direction at lunch in a Mexican restaurant. (¡Ay, caramba!) I felt most sorry for the young guy serving us who wanted to tuck, duck, and run away with our enchiladas. It was totally embarrassing, really uncalled for, and legitimately landed my man a turtled Beadcatcher. I told him I was giving him a three-day Beading time-out. There wasn't much discussion about it, because when a man has really shown his ass, he is generally all too aware of it. Which, in this situation, is kind of nice because a lot of times you get to skip the whole lengthy explanation as to *why* the Beadcatcher is getting turtled.

So I gave him three days, but if memory serves, he delivered such a stellar about-face that I abbreviated his Beading suspension by inviting him to drop a Bead. Other Beaders have had to hand down more lengthy turtling terms, but once the sentence was served, they righted their Beadcatcher and moved on. An important thing to remember is that once you right your Beadcatcher, you move on from the offense—you leave it behind. The Forty Beads Method is about creating that onward flow in your marriage, so keep an eye on your Beading partner and at the first sign that the situation is improving, when you feel even an inkling of something positive for him, go ahead and invite him to drop a Bead. Important: Keep in mind that turtling is a Beading move to be used only when you *really* need it. Don't pull it out too often, because if you do, and this is pretty obvious, there's really no point to your Beading practice.

THE FORTY BEADS CREED :: RULE #7
Don't Get Cocky
Never abandon the Bead—even when you *know* you're a Beading expert.

❁ DON'T ABANDON THE BEAD

At a certain point in the Beading process, you might feel so confident in the strength of your relationship and your Beading expertise that you might consider abandoning the Bead. Don't. You might think that the Bead has served its purpose and that you can just let it go. Don't! It's such an easy trap to fall into, and it's just human nature. As soon as we *finally* fit into our skinny jeans, we toss out the whole "eating healthier" routine that made it possible for us to comfortably button up to the top. Until we need it again. If you find that The Forty Beads Method works really well for your relationship, stick with it. Just because you've formed a nice habit of getting down with your husband on a regular basis doesn't mean you don't need reminding—we all do.

❁ BEADING MANTRA #3
I Abide in the Bead

Repeat this to honor the Beads and the positive impact they have on your relationship.

The Bead is a physical reminder that both of you can see and touch. The Bead is there for you—keeping it real and within the parameters of what works for you—sort of like those guard rails in the bowling alley they put up so kids don't fling their balls all over the place. The Bead keeps you on the path of maintaining a great relationship. Even the most experienced Beaders, Beading gurus who have nailed The Method and practice with unfailing consistency, never abandon the Bead. Like recovering alcoholics, every good Beader knows we're all just one sip away from slipping back into our old destructive, sex-withholding ways. So when that tricky little voice in your head says, "We got this shit down—we don't need those Beads anymore," find your book and reread this chapter. It will be the 12-step equivalent of meeting your sponsor for coffee at the corner diner.

✿ HOPPING BACK ON THE BEAD WAGON

Even with all the nifty tricks, back-ups and do-overs I've explained in this chapter, the truth is that sometimes you will make mistakes. You'll fail to notice a Bead that's dropped or you simply won't be so prompt about getting around to it, and that has to be okay.

> *"Sometimes you will fail to redeem a Bead. You will have to begin again. You will have to reinvigorate yourself and one another. You will have to forgive yourself and your husband when the rules of the game aren't met, but the beautiful thing is that you can start over, and every red Bead is an opportunity for that possibility. And isn't that, at its most basic level, what a healthy marriage is all about?"*
>
> —ISABELLE

Well, *I* certainly think so. And just to be clear, starting over doesn't mean going back to Bead number one. It's about picking up where you left off—getting back in the game. A healthy relationship is about falling out and falling back in together—looking for those opportunities to turn everything around and taking them. "Sorry" can taste terrible when it's rolling off your tongue, and forgiveness? Well, that's a holy practice unto itself, but without forgiveness, all our marriages would be totally screwed.

So if and when you mess up, forgive yourself, and forgive him for the stomping contra dance he does on the bedroom floor while announcing your Beading negligence. Don't stay in the drama of that—just dust off your Beadcatcher, express remorse, and redirect your man to his Bead stash. The conversation about sex in your marriage is already out there—that's one cat you can't wrangle back into the bag—so use that to your advantage and just ask him to start dropping Beads again. Say something like, "Yes. I screwed up and I'm sorry. It was not my intention, but it happened. Please forgive me and Bead me as soon as possible." What man could say no to that? The Forty Beads Method is not a plan where if you screw up, you have to turn in your Beads—no way. All you have to do is get a running start and jump back on the happy Bead wagon. It just takes one red Bead—dropped, then redeemed—and you're back in the rodeo, cowgirl.

One last thing about abandoning the Beads? Some of you will. For good. That's okay. Some marriages are way more complicated than others, and for one reason or another, The Forty Beads Method won't work well for certain situations. The Forty Beads

Method is just *one* way. It's not the *only* way, and it might not even be the *best* way for you. But for me and other women who've tried it, it is a way we've found to deepen the relationships we have with our husbands. P.S. I sure hope it does work the magic for you.

✸ SHARING THE BEAD

When your Beading practice gets under way, you're probably going to be pretty fired up about the changes The Method is creating in your relationship. Some of you will hold this excitement tenderly in your heart, while others of you, who tend to be a bit more like me, will want to tell all your friends about it so that they, too, can reap the benefits of using The Method. Here's something to keep in mind: Some of your friends will love it and want to get started Beading right away, while others could be offended by the very thought of it. Some women will hate it. Incidentally, some women who feel threatened by the idea of The Method might try to pull a little subversive move on you by saying something like, "Oh, *we* wouldn't need something like that. Our marriage is great," thereby implying how unfortunate it is that your marriage needs work. Don't get sucked into this sad, sticky web. The fact is, *every* marriage has room for improvement—in one area or another—and those who refuse to admit it today will likely be dealing with the aftermath of their delusions tomorrow. Maybe that's a little harsh, but you get the point.

Some women will find The Method preposterous, explaining that they couldn't possibly find the time to work a Method like this into their busy days, since they hardly ever have enough time to have sex with their husbands as it is. That's cool. I totally agree—The Method wouldn't work for someone who stands squarely against it. I'm not into converting those who aren't interested in a marital conversion experience. That would be a waste of everybody's time. Henry Ford said it best: "Whether you think you can or you think you can't—you're right." And that's absolutely true—especially as it relates to using The Forty Beads Method. Whether you think it will be effective or you think it won't be effective, therein lies the story of your Beading success. I made that one up.

Suffice it to say that if and when you do spill the Beads, you might want to brace yourself for the varied responses you could get—which for me and a lot of my Beaders can be tons of fun. You know I've got a bunch of stories, and here's one about what happened when The Forty Beads Method wasn't exactly embraced at first blush:

One night, my husband and I ducked into our favorite restaurant to have a drink with some friends before dinner. They were on a triple date with two other couples we didn't know. Let's just say that these women proudly counted themselves among the buttoned-up variety of Southern women. It drives my husband crazy, but whenever I sniff out a tight-ass, I make it my mission to scare the hell out of them. I'm not proud of this, but it is sort of a trademark move I've developed over the years. As I sat perched on a bar stool, I began telling the ladies all about The Forty Beads Method. It was loud in the crowded bar so I had to speak up to be heard:

"So he just puts a Bead in the bowl by my bed, and that's how I know he wants to get laid," I said.

Those girls got pretty uncomfortable pretty quick, ducking and cocking their heads to determine if their husbands (definitely within earshot) had heard what I'd said. The blonde began speaking to me using her *inside voice* hoping that would cue me to turn down the volume:

"Well, that's just crazy," she said in her thick Southern drawl. "I wouldn't want him thinking he could have it every time he wanted it. That would mess up everything."

"Okay," I said, popping the olive from my martini into my mouth and extending my glass to my husband for another. "But it's working out pretty well for me so far. I'm just saying."

Right about that time, the hostess came over to let them know their table was ready. This was a good thing, since I'm pretty sure those girls were about to club me over the head and throw me out into the alley.

I mention the above story only to impress upon you how important it is *not* to let other people (particularly other women) negatively impact your Beading practice. Whether other people find your Beading practice intriguing or repelling is really not important. If any negative vibes do come your way, just let them bounce right off you, and remember that the naysayers are probably just jealous. Beading couples are sexy as hell, and what's more enviable than a great marriage?

27

· · · · · ·

Opening Pandora's Box

I know that The Forty Beads Method can feel a little intimidating at first, and I'm sure if you tried, you could come up with lots of reasons not to try it. After all, we are talking about opening Pandora's proverbial box here, and you may be worried that some kind of sexually charged pandemonium could break loose in your house, or specifically, in your bedroom. Maybe you're concerned that you could inadvertently be offering yourself up as a new recruit for the sexcapades. While those are valid reasons for feeling apprehensive, it's not all that likely that you're going to have an uncontrollable, raging sex fiend on your hands, and here's why: That heavy sack of Beads represents the guarantee of a whole lot of sex in his future. He can prove it—he's got the Beads right there in his dresser drawer. Tucked away in their ample state, those Beads magically take away his sense of urgency around getting enough sex. No urgency means no compulsive, fear-based preoccupation with securing the deed itself.

Okay, so he's not going to flip into this revved-up sex maniac once you begin using The Forty Beads Method, but you might see a little of that behavior at first—depending on the dude and his previous level of sex deprivation. In the very beginning, he may act a little like that fat kid in *Willy Wonka and the Chocolate*

Factory—he's gonna want some candy. There is the possibility of some initial gluttonous behavior, but I can assure you, it's only fleeting. What's way more likely is that your guy will be very careful not to abuse his good situation. I mean, only a fool would wear out the goose that's laying the golden Beads. One husband called them "Beads from heaven." That's a pretty accurate description. He followed that up with an extended explanation to his wife on how he intended to "respect" the Beads. Smart man—and he came to this *before* being presented with the *Pre-Beading Covenant*. (We'll get to that.)

You're not selling yourself into in-house prostitution here, and the good news is that once he truly understands that you're committed to The Method, a nice little pattern will emerge. That will be your new sexual status quo. And yes, it is likely that the frequency of your sexual encounters will increase, but not really by that much. Here's the thing about that: The frequency typically increases enough so that he feels totally taken care of, but not so much that you feel sexually put-upon, because the benefits to the relationship (see Part 6: The Beadefits) will far outweigh the inconvenience of one more time per week. An important thing to remember is that you're creating some major change in your relationship here, and you don't get to experience that by doing absolutely nothing. Here's your last Beading mantra (yeah, it's a twist on something the great Mahatma Gandhi said):

BEADING MANTRA #4
I Bead the Change I Want to See in My Relationship

Honestly, I haven't had any Beader complain that increasing the amount of sex in their marriage wasn't worth the positive impact it had on their relationship. So while the frequency of your sexual encounters will likely go up in varying degrees, depending on how much sex you're having now, your level of satisfaction with your relationship will grow exponentially. And as this happens, you might even experience some change in the form of personal growth. One really insightful and conscious Beader noticed that as the amount of sex in her marriage increased, a band of voices in her head started kicking up a fuss in an effort to thwart the positive changes coming into her life.

"I could feel some part of myself saying, 'Why do I have to redeem that Bead? Why should I?' I've called the Beads some pretty awful names, but in the end, I've kept to the course and realized something really valuable about myself: When I start making changes, some part of me emerges and tries to keep me stuck. This has been a pattern for me in my life, but the Beads have helped me break free of that."

—JESSICA

I find that really interesting. I swear I've learned so much about The Forty Beads Method from the amazing women who are using it. The Method is sort of like an onion—it's got a lot of layers that you peel back as you go.

So back to Pandora's box and the concerns that some new Beaders have around tossing their man the Beads. "What if I give him the Beads and I don't get any back in my Beadcatcher? That would kill me," one Beader confessed. If that's a concern, there could be one of several things going on. First of all, a wife who believes her husband has a lower sex drive than most men *could* have a hubby who's engaging in a little self-protective behavior he's learned from years of getting denied more often than not when it comes to sex. Kind of like a turtle that curls up into itself when it's about to get trampled. Some guys find ways to redirect their sexual attention away from their objects of desire because getting denied is such a strong and painful possibility. And of course, when we're not looking, they're taking matters into their own hands. Who could blame them? It happens, but the good news is, this is a problem that's totally reversible with the Beads. If this is the case in your marriage (and you know if this is the case in your marriage), giving him the Beads will heal his emotional scarring around getting the consistent shove-off. For this reason, getting Beads in your Beadcatcher shouldn't be a problem.

A second reason a Beader might fear a lack of Bead return could have to do with medication. Men who've got some antidepressant, anti-anxiety, or high blood pressure meds on board *do* oftentimes experience a lull in their libido. Men really hate something messing with their ability to get the blue steel on, and as it turns out, Beading can be really great to help with that, too. I'm not saying The Forty Beads Method is some kind of cure-all that can shake a man out of a clinically depressed state, but remember how guys have this automated response to sexy images and how anticipating the deed is a big part of the fun for them? Well, that's why Beading can ramp up a guy's sex drive that's getting stomped by some drug. It's the combination of him anticipating having sex and imagining having sex, which naturally follows a Bead drop, that gets his loins fired up instead of letting them lie dormant during stressful or difficult times.

"My husband struggles with anxiety. When he's having an intense anxious episode, he has to take an anti-anxiety medication that makes him less interested in sex. He's always hated this and it has created its own set of problems in our relationship. Beading has really changed this situation for us. I asked him about this once during an episode and he said 'The Bead helps me *get going* when I have to take that stuff.' I think Beading makes him feel more like himself even when he's not feeling much like himself."

—ANITA

I love that. Nudge Cards can be helpful in these types of scenarios. You may feel like he needs a little kick in the pants to get him going—so drop a Nudge Card and invite him to drop a Bead. Dropping a Nudge Card can convey the message that "Yeah, I know things aren't exactly right for you right now, but I still want you." Who doesn't love that kind of unconditional support?

So if you're worried about getting Beads too often in your Beadcatcher or concerned your Beadcatcher will collect dust, neither one is a good reason not to try The Method—not if you're really interested in creating some meaningful change in your marriage. Like one happy Beader said, "Why would you *not* Bead? I mean, nothing bad can come of it." And that's really been the case—so far, anyway. We have had a couple Beaders come up pregnant, but in their situations, that was a good thing. So a little nervous energy is completely normal when taking up The Forty Beads Method. You are no doubt stepping out of the box when you commit to The Creed, but when you're ready, the best thing to do is just gather your courage, suspend your fear, and jump on in. Sort of like "Leap and the net will appear," but it's "Toss the Beads and your marriage will soar." Doesn't that sound fun? It is.

Some couples need a little extra assurance that each party will stick to the plan as The Method lays it out. A lot of women insist that, while they *are* willing to give The Method a shot, they know for a fact that *their* husband will either (a) dump all the Beads into their Beadcatcher at once or (b) drop a Bead every single day, thereby rendering her exhausted and completely pissed off.

On the flip side, a lot of men, while overjoyed by the offer to begin Beading, question whether or not their wives will actually follow through. By the way, I'm absolutely sure my husband was one of them, but, patient man that he is, he didn't voice his skepticism and opted instead to ride it out for as long as it lasted. Smart man, don't you think? So to address this concern, which really boils down to trust, I thought signing some kind of agreement before getting started might be helpful. Hence, The Forty Beads Pre-Beading Covenant you'll find printed here. It's on a page all by itself so you can photocopy it and both sign it, notarize it (just kidding, although some Beaders have!), and tuck it away for safekeeping. This Covenant clearly spells out each Beading party's intention for his or her Beading practice. Intention is really important. I believe that the success or failure of *any* endeavor is based on the intention that is set from the moment the venture begins.

THE FORTY BEADS PRE-BEADING COVENANT

I, _____, promise to respect
the Beads.   (MALE BEADER)

I will not squander the Beads by engaging in compulsive, incessant Bead dropping, as I understand that this would surely wear out my Beading partner and lead to a swift and justifiable termination of my excellent situation. Herein lies my intention.

_____   _____
     (MALE BEADER)   DATE

I, _____, promise to respect
the Beads.   (FEMALE BEADER)

I will acknowledge and redeem each Bead that is dropped within the allotted 24–hour redemption window with the very rare exception of sickness, natural disaster, or true asshole behavior on the part of my Beading partner. I understand that failing to redeem each Bead in a timely fashion would render this practice ineffective and would surely and justifiably disappoint and piss off my Beading partner.

Herein lies my intention.

_____   _____
     (FEMALE BEADER)   DATE

28

......

Situational Beading

There will be certain situations that crop up that may threaten to interfere with the Beading process. I think there's a word for these events that throw you off the course of your normal routine. What's the word? Oh yeah, "life." The Forty Beads Method isn't like a lot of plans where if you mess up, for whatever reason, you're totally screwed and have to start all over again. With Beading, if you get off track, it just takes one little Bead to get you back on track. Here are some examples and suggestions for Beading in potentially compromising scenarios.

❁ BEADING AWAY FROM HOME

Okay, so I guess certain vacations are more conducive to Beading than others, and there are a few types of getaways that involve exceptionally tight quarters where the benefits of Beading are overshadowed by the potential consequences of getting caught in the act. Yikes. The family camping trip is one. Sharing a tent with your kids would likely necessitate a suspension of Bead play.

But there are other types of family vacays where continuing the Beading process makes a lot of sense and will make the trip that much more enjoyable, and where leaving the Beads behind could be a bad idea. I learned this one the hard way on our annual trek to the north woods of Canada during our first summer of Beading. I thought it would be silly to take the Beads along—especially considering all the necessary shit we *had* to take. I figured we had this Beading thing down—and *hello*, I did make it up, so surely we could coast for a couple weeks Bead-free. That was when I became the very first overly cocky Beader. It's not that we didn't do it on the vacation at all, but sex definitely got knocked down a few rungs on the priority ladder. What with organizing sailing lessons for the kids and family cookouts, a week into the vacation we felt less connected.

Here we were, the two of us, sleeping in our own cabin hanging over Lake Huron (which brings with it certain expectations), and we'd gotten so sucked into what everybody else needed from us that we forgot what *we* needed to maintain our great relationship. Life had gotten in the way—even on vacation. And maybe it happens *especially* on vacation when we're busy busting our asses creating photo album–worthy memories. So a word to the wise Beader: Whenever you can, take those Beads with you. One of my Beaders told me that she and her husband had a blast with the Beads in Costa Rica—*¡Pura Vida!*

❸ BEADING WITH A TRAVELING SPOUSE

Whether the traveler is you or your husband, maintaining an effective Beading practice can take some effort—especially if one of you is gone half the time. Just staying married takes a ton of effort when one person is on the road a lot. There are a couple of reasons for this: First, when there is not a lot of couple or family time, there can be a lot of pressure on each spouse to make that *together time* perfect or some version of perfect. Pressure is stressful, and stress breeds conflict. The second thing, which actually folds back into the first thing, is that sometimes it's hard to feel connected to someone you haven't laid your eyeballs on for days or weeks. And if kids are involved, there could be some resentment on the part of the one who always gets left behind propping up the fort for the family while the other spouse is off, likely busting his or her ass, but away nonetheless. Given these reasons, sometimes reunions are joyous, loving affairs, and sometimes coming back together can feel more like you're trying to re-enter the Earth's atmosphere. There can be unspoken questions like "Where the hell have you been?" or biting commands like "Get your ass in here and contribute!" bouncing in between you. Beading can help you skip a lot of the not-so-great emotional conflicts involved in getting your relationship back on track. And sure, I know if you're the one left behind to tend to uh, *everything*, by the time he rolls in the door, you often feel like you're teetering on the brink and probably the *last* thing you want to do is redeem a Bead. Do it anyway. Remember how we talked about sex being "the great healer" and how doing it can clean-slate a bad situation? Well, sex is also great for righting a situation that simply feels *off*.

The most important thing I could say about Beading with a traveling spouse is this: anticipate, anticipate, anticipate. And that takes a little more planning on both your parts. He can't go dropping a Bead when you're slinging clothes in a suitcase, rushing off for a week-long business trip, and by the same token, you might need to get a jump on redeeming a Bead if he's about to hit the road.

If a lot of travel is the reality of your relationship, you might want to let him know about Beading by proxy right from the start. Using The Forty Beads Method with a traveling spouse can be challenging, but it's totally doable and definitely worth the effort, because when there's less time together, it really is that much more important that time spent together be good time. The Bead is there to remind you to focus on each other and your relationship when you are together.

✤ BEADING WITH A BUN IN THE OVEN

There are plenty of things to love about being pregnant and probably just as many things to hate about it. I loved that my breasts swelled to four times their original size. I hated that my feet followed suit. I loved that no one raised an eyebrow when I bedded down for my second nap of the day, and I really, *really* hated being totally sober at cocktail parties. Pregnancy is an intense time for a woman, because we've got a lot going on—mentally, emotionally, and physically. So it makes sense that we might develop an inordinate amount of fascination with ourselves, especially our bodies. With my first child, I took up bellybutton gazing as a full-time job. I mean, really, it is so impressive that we can create this tricked-out living space in our womb, sustain the life of our growing baby, and when it's time, push that newborn out into the world head-first. If we become a little self-absorbed, I think it's understandable—it's freaking amazing what we can do with our bodies. Suffice it to say that, like a lot of pregnant women, I had a hard time seeing past my own bulging belly and no doubt shoved the needs and desires of my husband behind the much more interesting bells and whistles on the newest Exersaucers and Diaper Genies.

There are many different stages of pregnancy, each one with its unique gifts and challenges. Maybe it's an out-of-sight, out-of-mind sort of thing, but once you've lost sight of your vagina, it can be hard to maintain much interest in it. When we're pregnant, sometimes we're just *not into it*, and an unsuspecting husband could actually be risking life and limb by making mention of the possibility of a sexual encounter. That said, other times we might be *really* into having sex—something to do with a bunch of blood rushing, you know, down there. I'm sure the hubbies stay pretty confused about it. For this reason and many others, my advice? While the doctor's giving you the thumbs-up, why not just Bead right on through your pregnancy? It'll keep you two more connected, and you'll be fortifying your relationship to better deal with the wonderful and challenging times ahead (i.e., wah! wah! wah!).

❀ BEADING AFTER THAT BUN BECOMES A BABY

Okay, there are the obvious physical limitations/issues. I still find it nothing short of a miracle that (most) everything went back to the way it was before I had my babes. Of course, all that takes a little while, and the dudes just have to wait it out. And if a husband has a problem with this limited-time, hands-off period . . . well . . . I can't even really get into that except to say, once again, that assholes don't get to Bead. So after your doctor gives you the green light and even if you feel like a sleep-deprived, skeeved-out zombie, get back to the Beads. If you do, you'll get to avoid the oh-so-common pitfalls of new baby couplehood.

I wish I'd been Beading after I had my babies. Babies are the best and really adorable, but they're also a *ton* of work. It's pretty common that marriages feel a significant strain in that first year after a baby is born. Nobody tells you that. What I did (and what a lot of new mothers do) was cut myself off from my husband, my partner in the whole baby thing, by totally ignoring him. Of course, I didn't do this intentionally and maybe it was just the screaming-squeaky-wheel effect at work, but ignoring my man when I needed his help the most wasn't the smartest course of action to take. When there's a new baby, more than ever, we want them to anticipate our needs—like fetching the burp cloth for us when we're covered in vomit *before* we have to ask for it. Beading can hook that up for you. I know that being a new mother is one of the most tiring experiences ever, but remember, a quickie can take less time than unloading the dishwasher and is appreciated way more by your man. Hell, when you redeem a Bead for a quick roll in the hay, *he'll* unload the dishwasher—while you sit with a cup of tea and watch him. It's not about manipulation; it's just about keeping the wheels lubed up and functioning properly in your complicated marriage machine.

❀ BEADING UNDER THE WEATHER

The Forty Beads Method is about spreading love, not germs. When one of you is sick, you don't Bead—you call a time-out, a suspension of Bead play. I don't know about you, but when my husband has a cold, I'm not snuggling up with him; I'm wetting him down with Lysol and germ juice. Of course, it goes without saying that once the infirm is back on his feet, Beading is back on.

❀ BEADING DURING SERIOUS ILLNESS

When a person gets slapped in the face with some serious illness, "business as usual" goes right out the window. Priorities shift, and attention is focused on getting the one who's sick well again. One really vibrant woman began using The Forty Beads Method while undergoing chemotherapy for stage-three breast cancer (she's thankfully cancer-free today!) and found it really helpful during that exceptionally challenging time.

"Beading brought our sex life back to the front line. It helped keep 'our time' a priority. Even with the crushing blow of my breast cancer diagnosis and subsequent aggressive treatment, I was still a woman who wanted and needed her connection to her husband to stay not only intact, but strong. With two young children (creating normal fatigue) and the side effects from chemo (creating crazy fatigue), Beading allowed us to take the guess-work out of when we were going to be there for each other."

—GRACE

As long as the one whose illness is putting them through the wringer feels up for it, Beading during a serious illness can be really helpful in keeping the two partners lovingly joined to each other (and when do you need each other more than during a difficult time?). By the way, as you learned earlier, having sex makes us release oxytocin in the brain, which makes us feel good and also boosts our immune system, which promotes healing. So if you can, when you can, when it's possible, Bead on.

29

......

Having Fun and Going Green

THE FORTY BEADS CREED :: RULE #8

Have Fun with Your Beading Adventure

Enjoy the fun, easy flow The Forty Beads Method brings
to your marriage.

The Forty Beads Method is, in essence, about having fun—in
your marriage and in your life. If it wasn't fun, I sure as hell
wouldn't be doing it. As I said in the beginning of the book, I
had no idea that any kind of method would emerge from tossing
my husband Forty Beads. But it did, and it's fun. More fun than
I've ever had with sex in my marriage. Remember when having
sex felt like you were getting away with something? Remember
when sex was something that you *wanted* to do, and not something you felt like you *needed* to do or *should* do? Well, guess
what? It can feel that way again. Once the negative associations
that attach themselves like nasty barnacles to your married sex
life are scraped away (no physical labor involved—it happens
automatically once you start Beading), a space is created for *getting down* on your list of fun things to do.

The Forty Beads Method takes sex in your marriage and

changes it from something you don't like to discuss or maybe fight about into something that's fun to discuss and laugh about. What follows naturally is that you both feel better about sex in your marriage. And it's not like putting lipstick on a pig. Once you start Beading, a genuine lighthearted feeling around sex begins to emerge. It's brilliant. Not me, what happens in your marriage, that's brilliant. A lot of women (especially the ones who were hesitant about trying The Forty Beads Method) are shocked by how much fun it is. Life is meant to be fun, and so is marriage. So have fun using The Method. And when you're doing something that's fun, you don't ever want it to end, right? Well, the good things is, the party doesn't ever have to end. Read on.

THE FORTY BEADS CREED :: RULE #9
Beader's Choice: Adopting a Green Bead Policy
If you're having fun, recycle your Beads.

Of course, it's a question I get a lot: "What happens when he's used all the Beads?" It's a logical question, and I've got an earth-friendly answer to it. The Beads are recyclable. If you want them to be. I mean, if you're enjoying using The Method, why would you stop using it? The Forty Beads Method is a totally sustainable method—one you can use forever—so after a Bead has been redeemed, don't throw it away, just tuck it into your underwear drawer or some other place he's not likely to go fishing around. It's all part of the master plan. Now don't go telling him that the Beads are recyclable right from the start. That's a little information you can keep in your back pocket until you're well into the Beading process and he only has a handful of Beads left. If you've kept your head in the game and Beaded down to just a few stragglers left in his pouch, I'd say The Method is working pretty well for you, and recycling should be a no-brainer.

He'll probably start bellyaching about his short supply, and that's when you can lay it on him that you've adopted a green Bead policy and replenish his Beads. That way, you get to relive the glory of the sexy, worship-worthy goddess all over again. I didn't actually have a re-Beading ceremony myself. I realized how well things were going, so my husband never came close to running out of Beads—I started tossing them back into his stash long before he could begin to fret over his dwindling supply. Recycling hasn't been a question for my fellow Beaders, and I hope it won't be for you, either. If all goes well, you won't be able to find a reason to stop Beading, because when you come across something that enhances your life in such a big way, why would you choose to kick it to the curb? Recycling Coke bottles is good for the environment, and recycling Beads is good for your marriage. Have fun and go green.

Part 6

The Beadefits

This is my favorite part and the whole reason I've written this book. You might begin using The Forty Beads Method because you think it's a fun idea, but trust me, it'll be the Beadefits that will get you hooked. I realize that, on the surface, The Forty Beads Method seems like it's centered around simply making your husband happy. While it is true that a husband gets real happy when he receives the Beads, that's only the very first step of the Beading process. The Method is really about producing the Beadefits, those tangible and intangible positive by-products of The Forty Beads Method that benefit you, your husband, and most important, your relationship. A Beadefit is any good thing that comes from using The Method. They are the result of each partner getting more conscious about the other partner's needs and becoming more willing than ever to satisfy those needs. Beadefits come in all shapes and sizes and are different for each couple, but generally speaking, they're pretty awesome, since they fill in the holes that were there in your relationship before you started the Beading process.

The Beadefits flow naturally from the Beading process—they aren't coaxed, artificially extracted, or manipulated into showing up; they just emerge and create meaningful changes in the relationship. It's like this: Before you started Beading, he may have (likely not even on purpose) pushed your needs into the back of his conscious thought processes, just like *you* may have pushed his craving/need for sex to the back of your conscious mind. That's all over once you two start Beading. You both happily acknowledge your partner's needs—*you* see the Bead in your Beadcatcher and redeem it in a timely fashion, and *he* develops a conscious desire to please you, thereby preserving his good situation. And instead of becoming drudgery, the whole process perpetuates itself because it's so much fun getting your needs met on a consistent basis. The Forty Beads Method helps your man clue in and put into action what matters to you. It's that kind of focused thought that produces the Beadefits, and it's the Beadefits that keep your Beading practice alive and your marriage feeling right. Reader, meet the Beadefits. I think you're going to get along really well.

30
······
The Big Shift

From the moment you start Beading, there's a big shift that takes place in your relationship. I don't want to overstate it, but when this shift happens, it almost feels like your marriage has just gotten a shot of some kind of mysterious elixir or love voodoo. It impressed the hell out of me, and with every subsequent Beader's story, I'm continually amazed. The shift can happen at the moment you give him the Beads or a little later, once he's had time to come to terms with his good fortune. So first, there's the big shift and then come the Beadefits, which keep coming and coming until *you're* the one who can't believe *your* good fortune to be enjoying this superb marriage. The Beadefits show up and breathe new life into your relationship—sort of like opening up the windows and letting the breeze blow right through on a beautiful, perfect day.

A lot of Beadefits involve the little things. And I don't know about you, but I think the little things are way underrated. It could be a touch on the cheek when he passes by, the trash taken out and the bag replaced without your having to ask, or even that confidence that comes with knowing he's looking at your ass when you walk by. Basically, the Beadefits are about what happens when a couple feels really connected to each other—when the stress falls away and is replaced by pure love. They begin with your husband's behavior and involve him being that really good guy you know him to be and treating you the way you know you should be treated. It's no act. He'll be treating you like the goddess that you are because you tossed some Beads into his lap and magically made his greatest wish come true. Here's a perfect example:

"So I gave him the Beads on a Sunday night and the next morning I woke up late, and spied a Bead in my Beadcatcher. Curious why I was left to sleep until just past eight o'clock, I was feeling like I'd fallen down the rabbit hole as I walked into a quiet kitchen. 'Where are the kids?' I asked. 'Oh, I fed them and they're biking to school now,' my husband said as he finished unloading the dishwasher. You have to understand. I *always* unload the dishwasher. Not my favorite thing, but I do it—every single morning. 'What are you doing?' I asked. He had this happy little grin on his face and said, 'I got up early and I'm just helping out. I like to call it choreplay—you know, like foreplay, but with chores. You saw I dropped a Bead, right?' 'Uh huh,' I said, chewing on a bagel and piecing it all together in my mind. Could these Beads be the secret to life? I can't wait to find out."

—MORGAN

A husband kicking in more with the chores is just one example of a Beadefit that typically shows up for couples using The Forty Beads Method, but it's a pretty good one. For his book *Voice Male: What Husbands Really Think About Their Marriages, Their Wives, Sex, Housework, and Commitment*, Neil Chethik performed in-depth interviews with 70 men and surveyed another 228. He found that husbands who pitch in around the house get lucky in the bedroom way more often than the ones who pretend not to smell a stinky diaper or walk right past an over-full trash can. He also found that these husbands tend to be in happier marriages. I'm not the only one who sees a serious link between needs getting met, a healthy sex habit, and a rocking relationship.

Using The Forty Beads Method takes away all the negative tension around sex and makes room for some healthy, fun sexual energy. It works by empowering your husband to just put it out there when he's ready for some lovin', which does wonders for him psychologically, as it erases a lifetime of uncertainty and concern around getting what he most desires in this world. The Forty Beads Method creates a positive, self-perpetuating cycle where everybody gets what they want. You get the happy, helpful husband you always thought you should have, and he gets the ball in his court, which he loves, and he is more than happy to pay homage to the The One who put it there. It's all about everybody feeling like they're being totally taken care of. My husband's always saying, "I am one lucky bastard." It's true. He is. And I'm lucky, too.

Guys are equal-opportunity issuers of credit. Where before maybe you got all the blame for the not-up-to-par frequency of sex in the marriage, after getting started with The Forty Beads Method, you'll be taking all the credit. And why not? You've unlocked the secret of the contented male and in the process fashioned a fantastic marriage for the two of you with just 40 little Beads. You're amazing.

31

......

Trolling for the Moment
(and Holding That Thought)

Once you start Beading, what happens is that you both start looking for those little pockets of time that would work for a rendezvous. You may not realize it at first, but what The Forty Beads Method does is actually put you both on the same page sexually as you work together toward meeting the mutual goal of redeeming that Bead. He'll recognize those opportunities, because as a man, he innately has a keen eye for that sort of thing. What's interesting is that you'll start seeing those potential openings, because you'll be noticing the difference the Beading process is making in your relationship (and also because it's just not a good feeling to have a Bead hanging out in your bowl—remember the languishing Bead?). This might sound like an ancient proverb by Confucius, but "When the intention is set, the moment will be revealed." The nice thing is that it adds a playful element to your daily life together when you're both trolling for the moment, even in the back of your mind. There's a certain intimacy that comes when two people share a secret, and that's what you two will have—a sexy little secret. He'll love it that you've joined him in this search he's been on for, like, his whole life, and it's likely that you'll be surprised by how much you enjoy the process.

"I got home Sunday morning after being away and there was a Bead in the dish. I was shocked by how I felt when I saw the Bead. I was filled with eager anticipation the whole day. I spent a large part of the day thinking about him and what we were going to do and how we were going to orchestrate it. Kids were underfoot all day, but could I pull off a quickie somewhere? Or should we wait for them to go to bed and take our time? Turns out, he spent the day doing the same thing—we had our minds on each other the whole day, anticipating this great thing that we were going to share. I loved feeling that we shared a really special secret: that at some point during the day or night, we were going to be together. It was a great day."

—JULIE

So when you two are figuring out exactly when you'll hit the sheets, what's going on is that each of you are (separately and at the same time) holding an image of your next sexual encounter. That's some pretty powerful, creative stuff, and it's actually the stuff Beadefits are made of. Carl Jung wrote a lot about how images can enhance a person's life, which is why he was so interested in working with dreams.

When you hold this positive image of your husband, it brings good energy into your psyche and into your relationship. Of course, the opposite is true when you hold a bad image of him; any energy you have for your husband and your relationship gets squashed when you focus on a negative image. And by the way, as any good Jungian analyst knows, the human psyche only has so much room, and you can either actively fill it up with the good shit or passively let it collect the bad shit.

My mom, who happens to be a kick-ass therapist, has studied Jung's work for years and has taught me a lot about how powerful the use of images can be. She explores images in her dreams for personal growth, and she sometimes uses images so she doesn't slap the shit out of my dad. Here's an example. One day she saw my dad carefully lifting Liza, their feeble 13-year-old yellow lab into the back of his Suburban. Even in her last days, she still wanted to go everywhere with him. My mom said she fell in love with him all over again watching him that afternoon. So when he does something stupid that totally pisses her off (something he's developed quite a knack for in their 48 years of marriage), instead of ripping him a new one, she images him putting Liza into the truck, and it shifts her feelings toward him. Granted, this woman is pretty effing evolved spiritually, but we can do this, too, if we make that choice. And I have to tell you that when you sign up for The Forty Beads Method, it's sort of implied that you're willing to make some changes and better choices that will foster the kind of relationship you want.

Once you begin Beading, there will be the imaging that's centered around sex, and for you, there will also be imaging going on around your husband's really great behavior. From the moment you give him the Beads, he's going to like you a whole, whole lot. Not saying he doesn't like you now, but for sure he's going to like you more. And since guys like to do nice stuff for people they like, he's going to be doing all these sweet things— like bathing the baby or inviting you to relax while he puts the kids to bed.

"It's like The Beads opened up his ear canals or some altruistic part of his brain. He anticipates my needs and acts on them instead of pretending he doesn't hear me when I ask him to do something. I love that."

—ANNE

Your man filling your needs on a consistent basis gives you some sweet images of him to hold in your brain, images that bring you closer together, and you won't be left to focus on, say, an image of him sitting on the couch watching TV and scratching his balls. See how that works? Definitely a Beadefit, right?

And even if (okay, when) he does shove his hands down his pants during the big game, it won't gross you out nearly as much. In fact, you may not even notice, because when your man is acting like the great guy you know him to be, you'll automatically pay a whole lot less attention to the little stuff that bugs you.

32

•••••

Beading and Quantum Physics

According to quantum physics, everything in this world projects measurable energetic frequencies—even something as inanimate as a rock. As humans, we project energetic vibrations out into the world through our emotions and our thoughts. When your husband goes to his Bead stash, selects a Bead, and drops it in your Beadcatcher, that simple act creates a release of positive vibrations that swirl all around your relationship, based on the fact that you're a sure thing. These positive vibrations, which he experiences as love toward you, happiness, and delicious anticipation of the sex in his future, work together to deliver that guy you want to be with in every way.

So on any given morning, he could be looking in the mirror, straightening his tie, and decide to drop a Bead. As he drops that Bead, he's going be thinking, "I'm the man. I have a great life. I love my wife." And guess who gets to be the recipient of all that positive energy? That's right. That energy is completely directed toward you. How sweet is that? He's feeling all these great things about his wife and his life, and the great thing is, he's right about all of it. Because he believes these things to be true (because they are true) and he *acts out of these beliefs*, it actually *does* come to pass that he *does* have a great marriage (because he's behaving in ways that maintain a great marriage) and a great life. Does that make sense? Quantum physics can be a little slippery to pin down, but that's it in a nutshell—as far as our purposes go. One Beader bottom-lined it nicely:

> "He walks around like he just got laid. All the time. And let me tell you, that makes for one agreeable and attentive man. Like all women, I much prefer an agreeable and attentive man. I respond better to him and our relationship is greatly improved since we began Beading."
>
> —ISABELLE

The Forty Beads Method is about harnessing that "just been laid" energy—you know what I'm talking about—that easy feeling that your relationship is floating along on a puffy cloud of sweet adoration in the hours following a roll in the hay. The Method *captures* and *uses* that energy to benefit the relationship instead of letting it just dissolve into the atmosphere. It's a little like installing solar panels on your roof to collect the energy of the sun, but a lot less work. That positive energy is there in your marriage once you begin Beading—The Forty Beads Method ensures you make good use of it.

The Beadefits are born out of this energy. Just as you join him in looking for opportunities to slip in a quickie, he begins looking for ways to please you—like closing the bedroom door to let you sleep in while he takes the kids to school. Sound unlikely? It happened to me just the other day. When he's feeling marital satisfaction, he starts behaving in all the ways you really dig, which in turn gives *you* that feeling of marital satisfaction and makes you more than happy to redeem the next Bead that comes your way. See how that works? We may not be moving tectonic plates here, but we're shifting some major energy around in our marriages.

33

......

Gettin' Up for Gettin' Down

Timing is everything. And when it comes to sex, bad timing is the worst. So often when our husbands approach us for sex during our everyday ass-busting lives, bless their hearts, they just miss the mark. They think nothing of snatching us from the arms of Morpheus, god of sleep, with *the hand*, which might as well be a claw, right? Or how about this: You're hustling at the kitchen island slapping together peanut butter and jelly sandwiches, and he approaches you from behind and presses the length of his entire frame against you. Uggh! That's really not a turn-on, and while we might give them a polite little chuckle, mostly it just pisses us off. We don't like being caught off guard and/or being considered a bitch if we're not ready at a moment's notice.

The Forty Beads Method puts an end to those awkward untimely advances, and the nifty little buffer of time between Bead drop and Bead redemption gives us a chance to get ready for getting down. Getting ready means different things for different women. For me, it could mean opting out of that extra glass of wine that's no doubt going act like an Ambien in my system and knock me out at eight o'clock. A lot of women say they like having time to freshen up and feel sexy—maybe even shave their legs. It might also mean getting lunches made the night before so you can drop the kids at school early and get back in time for some morning action. Morning time is the right time, don't you think? We Beaders love our buffer of time.

"I came home from yoga class around nine o'clock—sweaty and exhausted. I saw I had a Bead in my Beadcatcher, and my first reaction was, 'Shit! That wasn't there earlier tonight!' Then I remembered that I had 24 hours to redeem that sucker. Over the course of our marriage, I've habituated this knee-jerk reaction to my husband's sexual advances, which has been 'No!' Well, the Beads are changing that for me. Now I have time to get mentally prepared for the Bead redemption *on my own*, without involving him in some confrontation over not wanting to have sex right then. This buffer of time gives me an opportunity to *choose* a positive reaction to his desire for me, which has done wonders for our relationship. So the next morning, I felt refreshed after a good night's sleep and was able to happily acknowledge the

Bead—knowing I would redeem it later that night. The Beads are melting away my bad habits and changing my marriage in the process."

—EMMA

A lot of us need time to mentally prepare for the deed—maybe like an athlete who runs a race in her head before strapping on her sneaks and hitting the track. Whatever kind of getting ready you need to do, using The Forty Beads Method gives you time to do that before you do *it*.

34

......

Beading Good Habits into
Your Marriage

Best-selling author Stephen Covey (*The Seven Habits of Highly Effective People*) says that it takes 21 days to establish an act as a habit. Once you begin Beading, it won't take that long for you see some significant shifts in your marriage, but it may take that long to really get into the groove of your Beading practice. Sex gets shoved off the must-do list for lots of reasons, but often it's just that we get out of the habit of initiating it, wanting it, or saying yes to it. And we all know that's a really bad habit for the health of a marriage. The Forty Beads Method is a guide that helps you and your husband get out of any negative sexual ruts you might be experiencing and helps you establish a nice, healthy sex habit in your marriage. And the more time you get under your Beading belt, the easier falling into bed with your man becomes. It becomes a habit, a good habit that continually feeds your relationship.

It may take 21 days or it may not, but one day you'll realize that you've reached a new norm as far as how often you're getting down with your husband, and you'll have some positive feelings about that new norm because you'll know it's the reason your relationship is so much better.

Just like everything else in this world, practice makes perfect, or damn close to perfect. So it just makes sense that the more sex you're having, the better and consequently more fun that sex is going to be. Generally speaking, and you know I'm not into talking about all the technical between-the-sheets maneuvers, I will say that having more sex does seem to give a person more access to their passionate side. That's another Beadefit. It's something like strength training for the love muscle; the more loving that's going on, the more those flames of desire get fanned and the coals of passion get stoked. So you don't have to become a Tantric sex devotee in order to feel the heat; just use your Beads.

And the thing about good habits? They tend to spread. So you'll have your healthy sex habit, and you'll also start seeing good habits in other areas of your relationship forming as well. That loving, best-foot-forward behavior that happens as a result of the Beading process gets established as routine and becomes the new, better way of treating each other. In other words, the Beadefits stick around because they turn into good habits. And what's great is that good habits go a long way toward crushing bad ones, in or outside the bedroom.

"I realized the other day that since we started Beading, my husband doesn't play those silly manipulation games around sex anymore. I think the games had become a habit for him over our 20-year marriage and once we started Beading, the annoying games completely stopped. I always hated those stupid games and now he doesn't need them anymore. What a relief!"

—EVELYN

So it's out with the old and in with the new. Go ahead and Bead some good habits into your marriage, and stamp out some bad ones in the process.

35

......

Taking Sex Off the Bicker Block

Another thing that The Forty Beads Method does is take sex off the list of highly flammable topics. We all have those subjects in our marriage that we just don't see eye to eye on, and I take comfort in knowing that my husband and I have one less contentious item to deal with on a daily basis. While money is the number one reason people fight and eventually get divorced, sex is a close second on the bicker block of most marriages. Who wouldn't be interested in finding a simple, fun way to avoid the world's second-biggest matrimony crusher?

Sex is just not something the two of you can fight about when you're a sure thing. When sex *is* an issue in your marriage, don't you do your best to avoid the subject altogether? I know I did. And even when you're *not* talking about it, there's this big purple elephant sucking all the air out of the room. Unless your man is really happy with his sexual situation, the words just get in the way when it comes to him initiating the deed. The problem is that by the time he's ready to talk about it, he's probably pretty worked up about it and won't be very eloquent in his delivery. He'll spit out something like "We never do it" or "It's been a really, *really* long time," both of which imply a lack of awareness or neglect on our part, and we don't like that. Once you've established a good Beading practice, the words can and will come back into the desire for sex, but without any negative tinge to them.

Not only does The Forty Beads Method take sex off the touchy-subject docket, it actually makes it something fun to joke around about. One Beader saw that her husband dropped two Beads at once. She knew he was being funny, so she texted him, "Should I invite someone to join us?" They got into this cheeky little threesome-inspired texting frenzy. That's fun, right? And if you've got kids, you'll probably develop some sexy Bead-speak to keep the babes in the dark about what's so funny. One Beader said that her husband will bring her a cup of coffee and say, "Do you like Beads?" and she'll say, "Why yes, honey, I certainly do like Beads. Do you like Beads?" Yeah, he likes Beads.

Once you've developed a tight little Beading practice, you two might start talking about sex in ways you never did before. Maybe you two will begin to discuss things you'd like to do differently between the sheets, and you'll both be cool with going there in a conversation, because it's fun to talk about sex when everybody's basically happy with their sexual situation. For example, one day my husband was like, "Honey, maybe you'd like to find something a little nicer to replace your browns." Doesn't everyone have a pair of browns? You know, those comfy faded cotton PJ's that get worn way too much. (I'm wearing mine right now.) He didn't say it, but I knew he was thinking how nice it would be if I came at him to redeem a Bead and wasn't wearing those old pajamas. I got it—not a problem. Maybe he's working up to asking for some silky tap pants and a red wig. Baby steps. Here's what some newlywed Beaders had to say about how The Method has inspired their pillow talk:

"I love how [The Forty Beads Method] has opened up the dialogue about sex in our marriage. We haven't been married very long, so it's been good to talk from the start about something we might have avoided discussing for years."

—LOUISE

That's sweet. The bottom line is that only good things can come from talking more openly and more often about sex in your marriage. For those of us who aren't so new to the married life, taking sex off the bicker block can be a big step toward speaking a new language of love.

36

......

Hitting the Reset Button

Wouldn't you love to have a reset button you could push just when everything is turning to shit? A magic lever that pulled everything back into working order and maybe even cancelled out the fight you had the night before when you thought you just might rip your husband's face off? When you begin using The Forty Beads Method, it is literally like hitting the reset button in your marriage and getting a fresh start every time you redeem a Bead. What's more valuable than a clean slate? The Method works by continually pulling you back to what's important. Every time you redeem a Bead, it's like you've re-upped the agreement you made to maintain a great relationship with your husband—at least that's how he'll see it. And you'll see it that way, too, because every redeemed Bead enriches your life together.

Do Beading couples live happily ever after? Well, yeah. Happily ever after with all the twists and turns and bumps in the road that life has to offer. The difference is that Beading couples handle those difficult times much better and come back together way quicker than before they started Beading. I call this impressive post-conflict turnaround time the "Beading boomerang effect," and it's created by the new, different kind of strength your relationship has developed.

"Beading has made my husband more *tuned in* to me after he does something stupid, instead of being defensive and stomping off into his own corner. I'm pretty sure this is because he wants to be on the ready when he's all clear to drop a Bead—he's looking for the moment when he can come back to the party. The Beads offer a nice entry point back to the party where there's no pressure on either side."

—JESSICA

That works, right? Over time, the Beading process creates this stronghold, this undeniable—almost tangible—connection between you and your husband. It instills a "we're good" kind of confidence in your marriage that is present all the time. Other things foster confidence in a marriage too, like a shared history and children, but somehow, Beading slaps an additional layer of irrefutable contentment, stability, and satisfaction onto the relationship. And it takes a lot to shake that. Getting a well-established Beading practice going will turn you two into the Teflon couple. The bad shit might come at you, but it won't stick to you, and if it can't stick to you, it certainly can't bring you down. Now that we understand how and why sex is a healer, it just makes sense why The Forty Beads Method is so effective: It puts sex right out in front and uses it as the highly effective tool for peace that it most definitely is.

37

•••••

Him: Remembering Not to Forget

My husband and I had this psychiatrist for a few years. (Did I mention that we've run through a slew of them?) His name was Dr. B and he was fabulous—everything we'd always hoped for in a shrink and more. I still haven't forgiven him for retiring. Before he ruthlessly abandoned us, he asked my husband (who, at that time, had a tendency toward forgetfulness) a brilliant question— the $10,000 question is what he called it, and here it is:

"Ray, if I offered you $10,000 to meet me downtown on a specific corner at two p.m. on Thursday afternoon, and all you would have to do to get the money was show up, do you think you'd be able to do that?"

My husband looked at him like, "Am I really paying you two bills an hour to screw with me?" Dr. B *was* kind of a wise-ass, which was one of the things we loved about him.

Ray played along and answered the question, "Yeah, I think I could do that, Dr. B."

Of course, the point that Dr. B was making with the $10,000 question is that, given the right incentive to *remember*, a person *won't forget.* When a guy forgets something, he'll have a whole host of reasons why he was unable to remember whatever it was you asked him to do. Something happened at work, he took a different route home, or, my personal favorite, you didn't call to remind him.

One of the more magical Beadefits to using The Forty Beads Method is that it seems to pry open the memory function of the male brain. It hasn't been scientifically proven yet, but here's what seems to happen: Every time your man picks up a Bead, it's because he *remembers* that you're a sure thing. When he drops that Bead in the bowl, he *remembers* that you rock his world. When you actually redeem that Bead, it becomes ever so clear that what he suspected is actually true—you *are* the goddess of love incarnate. So all these reminders of how stinking great you are create the incentive he needs to give you the best version of himself, which includes, but is not limited to, a burning desire to please. We love that, don't we?

So if your guy has a tendency toward forgetfulness with regard to things you ask him to do, chances are that will change once you start Beading. He'll be way more likely to remember to pick up formula for the baby on the way home and to remember that you haven't been out with the girls in a while, and so he might suggest you take some time for yourself and do that. He may not always remember to put down the toilet seat, but I'm pretty sure that's a genetically engineered trait that can't really be altered.

38

······

Beading Him Out of His Man-Cave

In his book *Men Are From Mars, Women Are From Venus* John Gray talks about the differences in how men and women communicate. He describes how when a man is super-stressed, he "goes into his cave," or in other words, retreats and over time evolves into a complete asshole, lost in his own infinitesimally small world (my words, not John Gray's). What happens next? We get pissed off and repelled by this self-absorbed prick and avoid him like he's in the middle of a herpes flare, which he might as well be because there's really no chance we're gonna want to get next to something like that. Am I right? Can I get a witness?

So here's the beautiful thing: The Forty Beads Method works by actually keeping your man out of the cave in the first place. How cool is that? You don't have to go through the whole drama of prying him out of his self-imposed sequestration, because when you're Beading, he's going to stay connected to you—even when he's stressed. Remember what it takes for a guy to feel connected? That's right—sex. And when you keep on Beading during those difficult times you'll find that you both pass on through those rough patches a whole lot quicker than you would have otherwise. Chances are, he'll even see you as his *saving grace*, his emotional life raft in rough waters. That's sweet, right? So keep him out of his man-cave and de-stress your nest with the Beads.

39

Gettin' Good with Gettin' Down

Maybe the most surprising Beadefit for me and for a lot of my fellow Beaders has been how The Method has shifted our perspectives about sex entirely. We've talked about how, for us girls, sex can be just a pain in the ass, but when you consider that a quickie can take less time than pulling through a touch-free car wash and weigh that against the direct benefits to the relationship, it becomes a no-brainer.

"I actually timed it the other morning. We were in and out of the bed in seven minutes, and it set a really great tone for the entire day. Before the Beads I would have said I didn't have time for that. I definitely have time now."

—ANNIE

What The Forty Beads Method does is remind you that sex is a no-brainer, a must-do if you want to enjoy the good life, which includes a really great marriage. That little Bead in the bowl gives the friendly little nudge we all need as we tear through our

crazy-busy lives, because it's just too easy to forget what's important. Once you get into the Beading process and experience the
changes that take place in your relationship, you'll get good with
gettin' down, too, because it's hard to maintain an ambivalent or
negative attitude about something that makes your marriage and
your life consistently so good.

40

......

A Beading Benediction

Okay, you bad-ass future Beader. You're ready and on your way. This is where the book ends and your adventure begins. I am pushing all the love and strength and determination I can hold your way. You now know everything that I know (so far) about The Forty Beads Method, and I invite you to make it your own. Follow the rules, but if you feel like it, make up some rules of your own. The Method is meant to be a creative one, so draw outside the lines and paint your own experience with the Beads. I'm going to go ahead and congratulate you on the beautiful relationship you're about to create (or enhance) for you and your man. And as I congratulate you, I want to also charge you with sharing the Beads. I wrote this book because I just had to tell you. Because I had a hunch that what works so well for me, my friends, and my fellow Beaders might work really well for you, too.

This is not some secret we want kept under wraps—it's a method that's meant to be shared. So tell your friends and neighbors. Pass the book around in the carpool line. I've shared many a Beading tip from the sidelines of a peewee football game. Tell your tight-ass sister-in-law who you think will probably hate it—you might be surprised. This book has the effect of creating instant intimacy and camaraderie among those who share it. Of course, as I mentioned, some women run like hell when you tell them about it, but judging from my own experience and that of my fellow Beaders, more women love it than hate it. We women need each other for support and inspiration, so host Bead parties—I'll come if I can. Sex is some pretty complicated shit, but when we drag our secrets and our concerns out into the light of day among friends, we realize that our situations aren't as strangely unique or as completely whacked as we originally assumed them to be.

I wrote this book because I stumbled across this Method, but also because somebody had to just come out with it—this truth about sex and marriage. I'll support you and let's support each other as we take it one Bead at a time, making our marriages the best they can be. Please keep me posted—send me Beadmail through the website, and jump on the Forty Beads blog to tell me and your fellow Beaders all about your Beading experiences. Here's to you. May you BEad Well and BEad Happy always.

:: Carolyn

START YOUR OWN
FORTY BEADS
❋ CLUB ❋

**Women getting together.
Changing their marriages.
Changing their lives.**

"I love my Bead Club. It's like book club, only we show up knowing we're going to get to talk about what's really going on—in our marriages and in our lives."

—LUCINDA

"Carolyn Evans invites you to exhale and realize that your marital struggles probably aren't that exceptional. Everybody has them and it's what you do [like use The Forty Beads Method] to overcome the struggles that makes the difference between a marriage that just survives and one that thrives."

—EMILY

"Bead Club? What's better than women supporting women in making their marriages more fun?"

—CELIA

GUIDELINES:

1. **Pick a good number.** Eight is a good number of women to have in a Forty Beads Club. Any more than that and it turns into a cocktail party with everybody talking over everybody else. If your goal is to share your experiences of using The Forty Beads Method, get feedback, and support each other, then you'll want to keep your group small. Of course, if your goal is simply to introduce The Forty Beads Method to your friends, then invite as many as you want.

2. **Pick the right women.** Fill your Forty Beads Club with women you like and who are at least somewhat like-minded. This may be obvious, but you'll want to put a little thought into who you bring into the fold. For example, your tight-assed neighbor probably won't make the cut. Then again, it's sometimes fun to throw in a wild card, since the The Forty Beads Method *can* bring out the adventurous side of your more buttoned-up friends.

3. **Get them reading.** Have all your group members read *Forty Beads* before the first meeting. Also pretty obvious, but pretty important. Just like you do in a book club, you'll want all your members to be on the same page when they show up for your first Bead Club meeting.

4. **Pick the right spot.** Don't set up your meeting spot in the kitchen where your family will circulate through for snacks and glasses of water (a likely excuse for an opportunity to eavesdrop). It's really best to wait 'til little ones are asleep. Your husband may camp out at the top of the stairs listening for something good—

can you blame him? Also, members should take turns hosting—
like book club.

5. **Have your members keep a Bead journal.** We think we'll
   remember that funny thing he said or that glorious Beadefit that
   made our day, and sometimes we do, but often we don't. Ask
   members to bring their journals for story swapping at Bead Club.
   White-knuckle moments? Hilarious husband behavior? That's part
   of the fun! Maybe even give a little prize for the best Bead
   story—vote by secret ballot at the end of Bead Club.

6. **Pick what you choose to share.** Don't spill any Beads you'll be
   embarrassed to acknowledge later. Bead clubs aren't professional therapy groups, and nobody's signing any confidentiality
   agreement when they walk in the door. That said, if you compile
   a group of women you know you can trust, then go for it—tell it
   all. That's what I always seem to do.

7. **Be nice.** Be accepting of the different types of experiences your
   fellow Bead Club members have. It's these different perspectives and experiences that make Bead Clubs interesting and so
   much fun.

8. **Meet once a month.** It doesn't matter what time of year it is,
   we're all crazy-busy. Once a month is often enough to stay connected as a group, but not so often that it's hard to make it
   happen.

9. **Once in a while, let the men crash.** I can tell you, they're going
   to want to come. They like to show up and strut their stuff, talk
   about how many Beads they have left—that's cool. Remember

how they like to compare? Of course, if and when you invite the guys, it won't be a real Bead Club night—just a cocktail party, and that's fun.

10. **Keep me posted!** If you have any questions on how to get started or issues that come up along the way, don't hesitate to email me at carolyn@fortybeads.com. And please send pictures so we can post them on the blog!

Epilogue

The experience of writing this book was like pouring water from a pitcher. I think it was so easy and fun to write because I've never been transformed by something so intensely—especially by accident—and felt so desperate to share it. I turned my manuscript in months early and over the last year, I've been amazed by the endless new implications, insights, and Beadefits that continue to emerge like green shoots from the trunk of The Forty Beads Method—things I've noticed myself or have been made aware of in feedback from my Beaders. What follows are just a couple of these "A-ha!" connections involving spontaneity and spirituality that I couldn't leave you without sharing.

I've been asked if the Beads might inadvertently squash the spontaneity in a couple's sex life and actually, it turns out, they have just the opposite effect. In the beginning of your Beading practice, it's partly the novelty of it that's stimulating, but what I've been delighted to see is that the longer couples use The Method, the spontaneity and creativity in their sex life actually deepens and grows. Spontaneity is a Beadefit that shows up as a gift to the committed Beading couple as a result of each partner having internalized the importance of moving their sex life forward in the marriage. As I've reiterated though out the book, to get your steady stream of Beadefits, you've got to stick to the rules about keeping your Beads in play, but there will be times when you just spontaneously fall into each other, carried by the moment. It's just what happens when two people are looking together in the same direction.

The connection between The Forty Beads Method and spirituality is a thread that runs so consistently thoughout the book that until recently I hadn't thought to shine the spotlight directly on it. The Method uses sex as a vehicle to create wholeness in your relationship—sometimes you've got to use the physical to get to the spiritual. We all crave this spiritual-emotional connection with our partners and in this frenetic, fast-paced world, it's so easy to forget the quickest, most direct route to wholeness. The Forty Beads Method is your reminder to continually tend the soil in your relationship so that those transcendent, soul-stirring moments between you and your husband spring forth again and again.

Plenty of books talk about personal enlightenment and creating spiritual fulfillment for yourself and of course, that's a crucial piece of the happiness pie, but it's been my experience that a Buddha grin dissolves pretty quickly when you can't stand the sight of the man you bump up against all day long and sleep next to all night. The Forty Beads Method is a feet-on-the-dashboard road trip to Nirvana that you take together. And just like working toward personal enlightenment, you don't ever get there and stay there—your soul needs consistent care and so does your relationship. This Method is about continually returning you to that point of loving, spiritual connection; and the best part is, it's always just a bead away.

Acknowledgments

Authors typically thank their spouses and go on about how they couldn't have written their books without them. With *Forty Beads*, this was quite literally the case. So thank you, to my husband, Ray, for your enthusiastic participation. You're the yin to my yang, I've loved you for as long as I can remember. To my Mom—it's not normal how much I love you. Your wisdom is sprinkled all over these pages. Thanks for jumping in with both feet because I could never have written this book without you. Thank you to my Dad—for wholeheartedly endorsing this from the start and for raising a female version of your raucous self. I thank my son, who at six offered to help me sell the Beads. Although I don't think I'll take him up on it, I appreciate his show of support just the same. I thank my daughter, who just turned fourteen, for working to get okay with her mom's book— you're way cooler than I was at your age. To Amy Hughes, my agent and great friend—thanks for sharing the vision and fanning the flame. To Jennifer Kasius—thank you for your discerning eye and for yanking me back when I tried to go too far. To Craig Herman, Seta Zink, Sandi Mendelson and Cathy Gruhn for making it rain. Thanks to Nikki Hardin, for years of friendship and steady support. To my early Beaders: From the bottom of my Beading heart, I thank you (and so do your husbands!), for your adventurous spirits, open hearts, and oh, so beautiful feedback. To the Forty Beads Angels: Mary Propes, Patrick Autore, R. Marshall Evans, Jr.—Charlie's Angels have got nothing on you. Your support is priceless and your timing, perfection. Thank you to everyone at Perseus Books and Running Press for taking *Forty Beads* to the people and specifically, to Chris Navratil, for getting the Bead rolling.

The *Forty Beads* Gift has every-thing you'll need to begin using The *Forty Beads* Method* neatly packaged in a handsome gift box ready to be given for his birthday, your anniversary, Father's Day, or anytime you're ready to begin your Beading adventure.

CONTENTS:

- one white, strengthened bone china Beadcatcher
- one leather tie pouch containing 40 crimson red ceramic beads
- three Nudge Cards (for optional use)
- one note that reads, "Our adventure begins the moment you drop the first Bead," with space for the giver to personalize for recipient

All housed in a vibrantly colored, hinged keepsake box.

Available at www.fortybeads.com, as well as at select retailers.

* The Forty Beads Gift does not contain information on how to use The Forty Beads Method—that's all in the book.